LAST
MEETING
OF THE
GORILLA
CLUB

LAST MEETING OF THE GORILLA CLUB

SARA NICKERSON

Dutton Children's Books

DUTTON CHILDREN'S BOOKS
Dutton Children's Books
An imprint of Penguin Random House LLC, New York

Copyright © 2019 by Sara Nickerson

Visit us online at penguinrandomhouse.com

CIP Data is available.

Printed in the United States of America
ISBN 9781101994429

1 3 5 7 9 10 8 6 4 2

Design by Anna Booth
Text set in Maxime Std

For the grandmothers:
Antoinette Violante Allen
Grace Carney Crotty
Florence Satoko Tachibana

LAST
MEETING
OF THE
GORILLA
CLUB

KLEENEX

The two things Josh Duncan remembered most about his very first day of school: He got a nickname, and he met Big Brother. The way the memory came back, all these years later and on another first day, seemed like a bad omen. If a person believed in those.

He tried to block out both—the nickname and Big Brother—by concentrating on details around him.

Look: a giant tree!

Look: a DEER CROSSING sign!

Look: a squirrel doing squirrel stuff in the middle of the road!

When those details didn't work, Josh tried to hum his thoughts away. That made everything worse.

"Why are you humming?" his mom asked.

"I don't know."

"Did you know you were humming? Or are you wheezing?"

"Humming."

"Are you nervous? Is that why you're humming?"

"Why would I be nervous?" Josh looked out the car window at the swaying pine trees and fuzzy green moss and lightly drizzling sky. "It's not like it's my first day of kindergarten."

First day of kindergarten: He'd had a really bad cold. The skin underneath his nose was red and raw from wiping. His mother was going to keep him home, but Josh had begged. It was his first day! Kindergarten! He was wearing his new shirt! He'd already brushed his teeth!

So he went. And it was fantastic. Until Book Circle.

At Book Circle the brand-new class sat on a blue rug while the teacher read a story about a hibernating bear. The rug was itchy but nobody squirmed. It was the first day, and they all sat with their backs perfectly straight.

The story was a good one, about a bear who slept in his den while other animals snuck in from the storm and had a party and ate his food. Josh loved it. It was the best he'd ever heard. It was so good that he leaned forward. Maybe (he's not sure but maybe) he even started to crawl, right into the circle. It was the picture of the bear's den that was pulling him in— all the shapes in shadowy corners.

When his nose started to run, because of his cold, Josh reached up and wiped it on his sleeve. He would have done that even if he hadn't been experiencing such fascination over the hibernating bear, and he probably would never have remembered it, except for what happened next.

Because right then, when he was wiping his big glob of green snot on his first-day-of-school sleeve, his teacher, Mr. Lombardi, looked up. "Joshua," he said, "in this classroom we use Kleenex."

There was a silence, and then one person laughed. That's all it took. Suddenly everyone was laughing and repeating, "Joshua, in this classroom we use Kleenex."

Mr. Lombardi clap-clapped his hands and chanted, "Class-class!"

They had just learned they were supposed to clap-clap back and answer, "Yes-yes!" but instead they kept shouting "Klee-nex!" and "Ooh, boogers!"

Kleenex. They said it on the playground at recess. In the lunch line. Chanted it. Whispered it. Made it into a song. *Klee-nex, Josh-ua, Klee-nex!* Someone started calling him Kleenex, and soon everyone followed.

Ruined, Josh stood by himself at the farthest edge of the playground. And that's when *he* showed up, slipping through some sort of invisible crack in the air. At least, that's how it appeared to Josh.

"Don't worry," he said. "They'll forget about it soon."

Josh pressed his back against the chain-link fence. "I don't think so."

"Trust me."

"But how do you know? And who are you, anyway?"

"I'm Big Brother," he said. "That's how I know. Big brothers always know."

And he was right.

Mostly right. Josh learned to walk close to walls. He didn't play kickball at recess or raise his hand in class. And he certainly never crawled into Book Circle again. And while his classmates did forget about *Kleenex*, they remembered *something*. There was a mark. Through first grade and second grade and third grade and fourth, there was a mark that set him apart.

But it was okay. Because he had Big Brother.

Until the day Josh dug a hole and buried him in the backyard.

MONKEY SMILE

Josh had stopped humming but was still thinking about hibernating bears and snot and Big Brother's burial hole when the Mountain View K–8 reader board appeared.

Smile! Picture retakes next Wednesday!

The announcement, in big bold letters, brought him back to the present moment, and the day he was about to face.

"That's good." His mother turned at the sign. "You didn't miss picture day." She maneuvered through the parking lot and slid into the No Parking zone, reserved for buses.

"I did miss picture day. No one ever shows up for retakes."

"Well, you're going to have to."

"You can't park here."

"I'm not parking. I'm dropping you off. Unless you want me to come in—"

"Mom! No!" Josh's nose tickled like crazy. Without thinking, he rubbed it with the back of his hand.

"Do you need a Kleenex?"

Josh shook his head. He wished his mom wouldn't have said the word.

"It's normal to be a little nervous."

"Not nervous." Kleenex. Kleenex.

"Your dad and I, we think you'll love it here."

Josh looked out the window and watched his new schoolmates, already three weeks settled. He saw them jump off buses and sling backpacks and snap onto one another like little magnet trains. His mom kept yakking about how great everything would be—the forests and lakes. Hiking. Skiing. "And Dad—he'll be back soon. And he'll call every night, to see how it's going."

She got quiet then. Josh was pretty sure she was thinking about all the boxes stacked in their new living room, the ones she would have to unpack herself while his dad was traveling through Asia, inspecting airplane factories. And maybe thinking about the job she needed to find. And how the grocery stores were all backward, with the cereal aisles not where they were back home.

His breath made a foggy spot on the inside of the window. When he wiped it clean, his new classmates came into focus. Some of the kids wore football jerseys, green and blue. "Do you have to be a Seahawks fan to go here?" he asked.

"We can ask."

"I was kidding."

His mom scratched her wrist, where a bumpy rash was creeping past the cuff of her sleeve. "Josh, listen. This is the perfect chance for you."

"Your rash is back. Why is your rash back if it's going to be so perfect?"

She yanked her sleeve and squinted past her son, to the mess of kids on the other side of the window. "I just want you to be happy," she said finally.

Josh stretched out his mouth, the way monkeys do at the zoo, when people stare at them through glass and want to believe they are smiling. After a moment, his mom smiled back. She opened her purse and rummaged around, finally pulling up a small white pack of tissues.

"Here," she said. Josh took the crinkly pack. His mouth went dry.

The last bus pulled out of the parking lot and the older kids straggled up the walkway, to the long buildings that made up the school. Almost all of them wore faded jeans and sweatshirts. Josh had worn a uniform at his old school—polo shirts and khaki pants—so all his jeans were stiff and new. And he was wearing a raincoat: bright red. His mom had picked it out.

A bell rang and they both jumped. Josh's mom grabbed his

arm and held on tight. "How about if I pick you up, right here, after school? The sky is so gray it looks like it might rain."

"That's okay. I'll walk like we planned. I have my new raincoat."

"Josh, honey. This is a great opportunity. Just—try and stay in the real world. Like Dr. Ted talked about."

Josh was sweating in his armpits, something new. When he reached for his backpack, his mother's clamped hand kept him in place.

He glanced at the rash. "I thought we moved here for Dad's job."

"We did. But it's also a chance for a fresh start. So I want you to remember a few things, okay? Are you listening?"

"I'm going to be late."

"Don't—" She was searching for last-minute mom advice. "Don't sneak your lunch into the library."

"You mean the haunted one, or the—"

"You know what I mean. And don't—" She searched some more. "Don't hum!"

With his free hand, Josh shut his notebook on the picture he'd been drawing. He wrestled his other one loose from her claw.

"And the biggest, most important one . . . Are you listening? Josh?"

Josh bit his lip. When would she stop?

"No imaginary friends. Right? You're almost a teenager."

That was it. "Mom! I'm eleven. I'm in fifth grade!"

"Exactly. That kind of play was fine when you were five. It was not fine when you were six, seven—"

"Okay, I got it."

"Don't even talk to *yourself*."

"Okay!" His chest. So tight. But he didn't want to use his inhaler, not right then with all that talk about all that stuff. The name Big Brother hovered in the air around them, but both pretended it didn't.

"Have a good day," she said as he opened the door. "Josh!" He turned. She held out the Kleenex. "You forgot this."

Josh shoved the Kleenex deep into his backpack and stepped onto the curb, where he stood and monkey smiled until the car was out of sight. Then he grabbed his inhaler and took his first real breath of the day.

FIRST IMPRESSIONS

Josh did have a first impression of Mountain View K–8. "Creepy," he'd whispered.

This was on the Friday before, when he and his mother had taken a tour of the school. Classes were over, the place was deserted, and the two stood outside on the gray walkway, waiting for the assistant principal to finish her phone call.

Mountain View K–8 was the complete opposite of Josh's old school, a redbrick building in the city. "I bet from a helicopter this school looks like a giant bug." Josh pointed to the long buildings that spread out from the circular center. "Those are the legs. And this is the body."

His mother glanced up, to the building above them. "So, what part of the bug is that? The shell?"

"That's not part of the bug. It looks like a weird, hovering alien ship." In his mind the weird, hovering alien ship was about to suck up the giant bug. "I don't know about this school, Mom."

"Joshua Duncan!" She gazed past Josh to the mountain that seemed close enough to touch. "Everyone else just sees all this beautiful outdoor space. This fantastic view." She took in a deep breath. "Smell that. Fresh mountain air."

"Yeah but you know what? That mountain is a dormant volcano. You know what that means? It could erupt." He shuffled in a circle, taking in the nature all around him—the grass and trees and bushes. "And why is everything so green? Don't you think that's weird? When everything is so green?"

"Remember, Josh: first impressions."

The assistant principal had tucked away her phone and was striding toward them with an extended hand and wide smile. "Good to see you again," she said to Josh's mom, and the two of them talked about the move: how it had been delayed and what a shame it was that Josh missed out on the first several weeks.

She turned to Josh and held out her hand. "Hello, Josh. I'm Ms. Yoshida. Are you ready to see your new school?"

Ms. Yoshida was chatty and helpful. She gave Josh a map of the school and pointed to the four long buildings—the ones that Josh thought looked like bug legs. "A, B, C, and D," she said. "Not the most creative names, but they work."

Josh studied the map while Ms. Yoshida explained that

the different buildings were for the different grades. "You'll mostly be in C," she said. "Although you'll move for Spanish. And PE is either in the gym or outside, depending. I'll show you that next and the locker room."

"What's the Hello Walk?" Josh asked. According to the map, it was exactly where they were standing.

"The Hello Walk is this wonderful space—right here." Ms. Yoshida pointed to the smooth gray circle with a border of benches. "And right above us is the old library."

"Josh thought it was the underside of an alien space ship," his mother announced. "Didn't you, Josh?"

The assistant principal smiled. "Well, the kids say it's haunted." She began to walk away, motioning for them to follow. "The new library is right over there, between the gym and the cafeteria. We call it the media center."

Josh heard her shoes clicking away from him, but he stood in place, staring at the underside of the old library. "Why do they say that?"

Ms. Yoshida stopped and turned. "What?"

"That it's haunted."

"Well . . ." She puzzled for a moment. "Just for fun."

"How do you get in?"

"There's a stairwell, on the other side of the Hello Walk. But it's closed to students right now. The new media center—"

"Ms. Yoshida—" His mother cleared her throat. "Why is this called the Hello Walk?"

"You know, the kids started calling it that, years ago, and the name stuck. It's our biggest covered outdoor space and a lot of students gather here at breaks. The playground for the younger students is on the other side of buildings A and B. So most of the older kids either go out to the playfields or they socialize here. It's a very friendly school, Josh."

Josh nodded but fixed his eyes on the map.

Ms. Yoshida looked up. "This old library will eventually be remodeled and repurposed, but until then we like to think of it as our giant umbrella."

"That's good," his mom said, scratching her wrist. "Isn't it, Josh? Because we heard it rains all the time here."

"Well—" Ms. Yoshida shook her head. "We call it liquid sunshine."

Laugh, laugh. Laugh, laugh.

On that Friday tour, while the grown-ups had laughed, Josh stared at the Hello Walk on his map, trying to imagine how it would look on Monday morning, packed with kids. *Hello, hello. Hello, hello.*

"What about earthquakes?" he blurted suddenly. "Did anyone think of that?"

They stopped laughing.

"There's a major fault line. With shifting tectonic plates"—
he motioned wildly—"all around! What would happen if the
earthquake hit while we were all just standing here? Underneath the giant cement umbrella?"

"We have drills," Ms. Yoshida answered calmly. "Earthquake drills. You will be prepared for any sort of disaster." She
pointed to the wide cement perimeter dotted with fat green
bushes. Everything was so *green.* "Or you can go around it.
Most of the walkways are covered. But you'll see. You'll meet
up with friends here. Sometimes there are bake sales."

Josh's mother shot her laser-beam eye message to *s-t-o-p*
and *f-o-c-u-s.* It was an amazing skill and froze Josh on the
spot.

It was true about the shifting tectonic plates: Josh had
done the research before they moved. But now, on Monday,
his actual first day, Josh knew it wasn't the thought of an
earthquake that was making his heart pound. It was the vision
of those kids, his new classmates. *Hello, hello.*

Another bell rang. Josh couldn't remember if it was the
late bell or the really late bell. Not that it mattered. He'd be
the new kid, walking in either late or really late. Probably really late, since no one else was around.

Right before he reached the Hello Walk, Josh spotted
the glass door to the old library stairwell. A sign on the door
said DO NOT ENTER. Josh tried to see past the sign, but it was

nothing exciting. Just a dusty gray entry and a flight of worn stairs. When he stepped away, though, he heard a voice.

"Haunted."

Josh shook his head, like an insect was buzzing in his ear.

"I know you heard me."

The voice made Josh's heart pound fast. Because it shouldn't have been there. It shouldn't have been anywhere, but especially not *there*, at that *school*, on that first *day* of a brand-new *start*. The voice made everything mixed up and muddled.

He began to walk quickly. Which one was building C? Everything looked like everything else. And where were the building signs? Josh swung his backpack around and fumbled with the zipper. He pawed through his notebook, searching for the map.

Where-where-where was it?

"Everyone is in class already." It was the voice again, familiar but older. "Not exactly the best impression on a first day, is it?"

This wasn't real. This wasn't happening. It was just because of Ms. Yoshida's joke about the haunted library. It was just about feeling anxious, and about his dad being gone, and his mom's awful rash.

Josh pulled out the crumpled map. With it came the pack of Kleenex.

Hello?

So Josh ran. On what was supposed to be the first day of his brand-new start, he ran. He aimed for the clear space between two buildings, far away from cement benches and bug-legs and the Hello Walk and a haunted library. Bushes and grass and trees blurred their terrible green all around, and his stiff new jeans made a rhythmic swishing that sounded like a whisper:

Run, Josh! Run, Josh! Run, Josh! Run!

Josh wanted to stop, but it was too late to go back to school. Way too late. Because "You only get one chance to make a first impression."

It was the truth. Josh had the poster at home.

SHADOW

Three weeks and one day into fifth grade and Lucas Hernandez was miserable.

Fifth grade was supposed to be the best year yet. Fifth grade, when his class moved across the Hello Walk, from the little kid side to the big kid side. When he and his friends could be on the playfields instead of the monkey bars. When they'd have real PE, and Second Lunch with the upper grades instead of First Lunch with a bunch of kids who still spilled their milk and spit out chunks of food when they laughed. Fifth grade at Mountain View K–8 was supposed to be a fabulous year. But it wasn't.

And there was only one reason: Maxie Moon.

She was back.

Lucas could feel Maxie Moon's eyes on the back of his head, boring into his skull like a dull but persistent drill. Even though his teacher, Mr. K, was being his usual best-teacher-in-the-world self, Lucas couldn't concentrate on what he was saying because of those drill eyes, pointed at him from the far-right corner of the very last row. It was like she wanted to get inside his brain!

While Mr. K jumped around in one of his rock concert T-shirts, most of the students laughed, raised their hands, and competed for his attention. But Lucas slouched low in his seat and attempted to calculate how many more miserable Mondays of the school year he'd have to endure. And Tuesdays, and Wednesdays, and—well, Thursdays and Fridays, too. But he gave up trying to figure it out. What did it matter?

Mr. K clapped his hands twice. "Ready-set?"

The class clapped back and shouted, "You-bet!"

"Okay, how's everyone doing on their Marvelous Mystery projects? Has everyone narrowed down their topic?"

Every hand in the class shot up. Every hand except one. Lucas hadn't even narrowed down his brainstorm sheet.

He'd been so excited when he first heard about the Marvelous Mystery project. They could pick anything—anything at all. And research it. And give a presentation. There was so much he wanted to explore. Big questions danced around in his brain, calling, *Pick me! Pick me!*

He wanted to know more about Stonehenge and alien life-forms and Bigfoot versus Yeti. Vampire bats and Venus flytraps and seedless watermelons—how do they grow when there are no seeds? There was the question of infinity and the question of black holes and the question of mummies. There was that neighborhood dog with three legs. Lucas wanted to know more about that dog and about everything.

Gravity!

Pompeii!

People in the circus who swallowed swords! How do they even do that?

His biggest worry had been how to choose between them all. And now, he didn't even care—about Marvelous Mysteries or soccer at lunch or the high school football game on Friday night or anything. Because she was back. And her eyes were drilling. And fifth grade was miserable.

Lucas turned to the window. A line of trees had recently been planted between buildings C and D, right down the middle of the center strip of grass. But to Lucas, even the bright green things looked soggy and gray. And then something ungray happened. Something red happened.

Lucas leaned forward. A boy in a bright-red raincoat was running down the center strip between the buildings. Sprinting! No, not so much sprinting. He wasn't the sprinter type—Lucas could see that right away. But he was going as fast as his legs could carry him. That was obvious, too.

He held his breath, waiting to see what the boy could be

running from. What would make a kid run like that? A wild three-legged dog? A zombie mummy from Pompeii? Lucas looked over his shoulder but Maxie was still in her spot in the corner, staring at him in her totally creepy way. The kid wasn't running from her.

Lucas glanced around the room. Was it really possible that no one else was seeing this amazing moment? He turned back to the window just in time to see something new. It was another boy, running alongside the kid in the red coat. This new boy was taller and faster and ran with ease. But no—Lucas blinked. It was just a shadow.

A shadow? But could a shadow be taller and faster than the person it was shadowing? Could it have a better stride? Lucas leaned sideways, as far as he could, until the red raincoat was out of sight. For some reason he couldn't explain, his own heart was beating fast. Like he'd been that kid out running.

He stared at the small trees, thinking about the boy's shadow. Usually he liked to watch the shadows the saplings made on the opposite building wall. But today—today there was not enough sun to make a shadow. Lucas pulled out his Marvelous Mysteries brainstorm sheet. At the bottom of his list he added a new one.

Shadows on a day with no sun.

BIG MOMENT

The voice had disappeared and the pants were no longer whispering, but Josh kept running. Because that was the plan that formed in his head as he was running. To just keep running.

Then what?

That didn't matter. Because he was running. And he would run across the field, all the way to the high school stadium on the other side. He would cross the football field and go around the fence.

No! He would climb the fence! Because this moment was bigger, it was grander than anything he'd ever been part of before. This moment was so big it was worthy of a musical score.

So he would climb the fence—No! He'd jump! He'd jump over the fence like a pole-vaulter, only one without a pole. And then he'd just keep running.

He'd run to the mountain, into the woods, and that's

where he'd live. His red raincoat was nearly as big as a tent—he would make a shelter out of it. In his backpack was a water bottle, and he had five dollars in his pocket, so he'd stop at a store along the way to buy provisions that he'd ration until he taught himself how to live off the land. Bread and candy bars and well, maybe peanut butter for protein. It was perfect. He'd also buy matches to build a fire. Or a lighter. Matches would get too wet in the rain.

He'd done his research to know that the Pacific Northwest had a temperate climate. There were wild blackberry bushes and tons of apple trees. Cherry trees. And lakes—he would teach himself to fish in all the lakes.

It was an epic plan, but when Josh reached the high school stadium on the other side of the playfield, he had to stop running. He stopped and bent over and gulped for air. And while bent over and gulping for air, he remembered that the mountain he was going to live on was a dormant volcano. And also that he had never gone camping. And also that he didn't like fish. So when he was finally able to stand up straight and face reality, he had one thought:

What

had

he

done?

Josh glanced back across the length of field he'd just

crossed, expecting to see Ms. Yoshida or a team of police offi-cers following him. But no one was there. On the other side of the soccer field was a baseball diamond, with a dugout. From where Josh was standing, the dugout looked like a safe little boat anchored in a sea of endless green.

And it *was* the perfect hiding spot. Dusty and old, but cozy and quiet. Josh slid down the solid wooden bench and looked out across the dirt diamond and green field. He clutched his backpack to his chest like it was a teddy bear and tried not to cry. For the first time that morning, he could tune into his own thoughts clearly, without the static of nervous chat-ter from his mother, or the mocking whispers of his stiff new jeans. With his mind free, Josh wondered if there was a way to fix what he had done.

Obviously he'd have to tell his mom.

Or

Obviously he'd have to go back to school.

Which scenario made him feel worse? He closed his eyes and imagined one and then the other. They were equally bad.

So he sat and waited.

He knew what he *should* do. He should go back to school. Check in at the office front desk. The people there would be nice. Like Ms. Yoshida. She would welcome Josh and help him find his classroom in Building C. That would be a responsible and good choice.

Another acceptable option: He could call his mother. He could tell her that this first day wasn't going according to plan and could she come and pick him up and take him out for a strawberry milkshake and maybe he could try again tomorrow? Or Wednesday? But that would involve finding a phone somewhere. Probably the school office. And what would he tell her, anyway? He imagined her at home, answering the phone, grabbing her car keys with her red, rash-covered hand.

No, he couldn't call his mom. Not until he had something good to tell her.

Josh hunched low, and that's when he noticed all the words—names—carved into the wooden dugout bench. Some were faint scratches, some were deep grooves.

Jase was here.

Natalie was here.

Ben and Emmett and Izaiah were here.

He imagined all the kids over all the years, sitting in the dugout, waiting for their turn at bat. Had they been nervous or afraid? Or had they been brave?

"I was here," Josh whispered as he traced his finger over every name. *Abby* and *Chloe* and *Jaxon* and *Maya*. "Joshua Duncan was here, too."

Just saying that made him feel less alone. He wondered if that's why people did it in the first place, wrote their names all over, like on walls and desks and freshly poured cement sidewalks. Public places, like bathroom stalls. Really public places, like freeway overpasses.

He didn't know the answer and didn't know how he would ever know. But seeing the names and tracing them with his finger made him feel better. A little braver. Brave enough to stand up and start moving.

THE LAST STOP

Josh cut across the playfield to the main road that led to town. He knew the rule: There was no leaving school without a note from a parent or guardian. If he did not show up to class, his mom would get a call from the office. It's what had happened at his old school on a regular basis, when he'd hide out in the bathroom or the storage closet. But things at this school were supposed to be different and he already dreaded seeing his mom's disappointed face when he walked in the door. Thinking about it made him walk slower. Why rush home to that?

The route was straightforward. Josh had practiced it with his mom over the weekend. As he walked through town, people gave curious glances before turning back to their cell phones and portable coffee mugs. That's when Josh got the feeling that he was watching himself, too, almost like he was a character in a movie. But it wasn't the right kind of movie, and he wondered about that. How do you get to be in the kind of movie you want to be in? Everyone else appeared to be in really awesome movies, full of camaraderie and laughter. Funny moments and ice cream cones. Adventure and suspense. Heroes! How could a person get into one of those?

Josh trudged on until there were no more stores and the tidy sidewalks turned to bumpy strips of gravel. There on the corner, right before the road forked and went into the forest, was a small store called The Last Stop. Josh and his mom had driven past the store several times already, and he always wanted to go in. "Look," he'd said, pointing at the sign. "Corn dogs!"

Now as he stood at the glass door on his messed-up movie Monday, the name of the store seemed ominous. It really *was* the last stop before the long stretch of forest road. He took a deep breath and pushed open the door. A bell tinkled above his head in a welcoming way, and the guy behind the counter looked up from his cell phone and smiled. "How's it going?"

"Good," Josh said, acting extra perfectly normal. The guy nodded and turned back to his phone.

The Last Stop was small but had just about everything in the world a person would need if it was actually their very last stop in the world, ever. Chips and buns and beef jerky and toilet paper were crammed next to strawberry jam and marshmallows and twine and bug spray. There was shaving cream and shampoo. Hair spray and cat food. Safety pins, baked beans, instant oatmeal, and ballpoint pens.

Josh wandered until he found the candy aisle in the center of the store. It had all of his favorites, along with the weird, nearly extinct kind of candy that might occasionally show up in a Halloween bag—things like Charleston Chews and Wax Lips and Chick-O-Sticks and Goobers. Even Pop Rocks.

Josh picked two PayDays, Twizzlers, a roll of Life Savers, and a package of Dots. He wanted the Pop Rocks but remembered a story about them exploding in a kid's stomach. Even though he knew it probably wasn't true, why risk it.

"Corn dogs are two for the price of one today," the guy at the cash register said, pointing to the glass case where golden corn dogs slowly rotated.

Josh placed his candy on the counter. "Are they good?"

"They are superb. Just like the ones you get at the fair." He took out a small paper sack and started ringing up the candy.

"Maybe next time." Josh looked to the far end of the counter where a display of Zippo lighters was propped next to a stack of bundled firewood and a small sign that said WORMS. The lighters and firewood and worms made him think of his original plan—to run to the mountain and live off the land.

"There's always that." It was the voice again, buzzing in his ear. "It's not too late for that."

The man handed Josh his bag of candy. "Try a corn dog next time."

And through the buzzing, Josh stammered back that he would, he most certainly would, he would even try two.

LAPS

Lucas was on the springy eight-lane track even before Coach Wolfberg, the PE teacher, showed up with her timer and clipboard in hand. Although the running unit didn't seem like it would be as much fun as soccer or basketball, Lucas loved the sprint across the playfield, past the baseball diamond and dugout, over to the stadium where the high school team, the Panthers, played their Friday night football games.

Bouncing lightly on his toes, like he'd seen the runners do on TV, Lucas turned back to watch the rest of the PE class trickle into the enclosed stadium. Some were running, some were walking. Fifth grade was the first year they could use the high school sports facilities. They also got to use the locker room to change into actual PE clothes, and even though those things made them feel big and grown up, Lucas noticed how small everyone looked next to the giant stadium and empty bleachers. A Marvelous Mysteries project idea fluttered around his brain, but he couldn't quite pin it down. Something about relativity? Perception? He wasn't sure.

"Hernandez," Coach Wolfberg called. "I expect to see you on the middle school track team next year."

Lucas grinned. The run over had cleared his head of all the weird stuff from earlier in the day, like the mysterious shadow and Maxie Moon. Plus, even though the sky was still gray, bits of blue were beginning to break through the clouds. He felt okay. He felt good even. He imagined he was the person on the poster hanging in the locker room. It was a poster of a runner, winning the race and breaking the finish-line string. Maybe that could be him next year.

Coach Wolfberg stood at the starting line while the class gathered around. She explained how the distance-running unit would work.

"Four laps around is a mile—" She had to stop there, to hold up her hand against the groans and complaints. "Hey, listen. You can do this! All of you! Four laps is a mile. Some of you may be able to run the whole way, and some of you won't. But you'll all get better, each time you try. I'll have a stopwatch going, so raise your hand when you're finished with your last lap and I'll call out your time. Then I'd like you to write your time next to your name. Eventually, your times will go down—"

"Coach Wolfberg, what if they don't?"

"What do I always ask of you kids?"

"That we do our best."

"Exactly. Any more questions?"

There were more questions, about having to go to the bathroom and dehydrating, what if they couldn't finish and what if the high school kids came out?

Lucas heard Coach say something about not starting out too fast. Something about pacing. But he wasn't worried like the other kids were. He had other things on his mind. Maybe, he thought, maybe things would be okay. Like they were before fifth grade. Maybe she would get tired of whatever she was doing. Maybe it would be like last time, when she finally just went away and left him alone. Lucas was so deep in his own thoughts that when Coach Wolfberg blew the whistle, he jumped. The run had started and his classmates had already surged ahead, like one giant rolling wave.

Lucas stumbled over his feet, but he righted himself quickly and found his way into the wave. It was a giddy happy moment for all of them, out there on the springy track. Full of energy and moving together, any one of them could be a track star.

But halfway around the first lap, the wave started to break up, and the kids who hadn't listened to Coach's advice about pacing themselves were already breathing hard. That's when

Lucas saw his opening and took it. He began to weave around bodies—to the right and to the left. While his arms pumped a strong and steady rhythm, his feet were like feathers.

"Go, Lucas!" his friends called out as, one by one, he zoomed past them. "Go, Lucas! Go!"

He leaned into the final curve of the first lap. His arms and his legs worked together like a perfect machine. He flew by Coach, who called out, "Looking great, Lucas!"

He heard her call out other names and knew that meant other runners were right behind, maybe even gaining on him. He picked up his speed. Running was giving him something he'd forgotten: a magical feeling of power and freedom. And that magical feeling helped push all the other thoughts away. He was unstoppable. Running could take him anywhere!

He flew around the second lap, and was turning the last curve on the third. When he glanced behind him, to see how close the next runner was, something in the stadium caught his eye. He looked again at the empty bleachers and saw the sparkle of her shirt.

Maxie Moon was there. At the very top of the stands. Watching him.

Lucas stumbled. This time when he righted himself his feet felt like cement blocks. All he wanted to do was get out of there, get off the track, run away to—somewhere—anywhere Maxie Moon couldn't find him.

"Pick it up, Hernandez!" Coach called out. "You got this!"

But Lucas knew he didn't "got this," not with those watching eyes. Still, he managed to make it down the length of the track, where Coach called out, "Just one more lap, Lucas. Finish strong."

One more lap? With Maxie Moon cheering from the stands?

Running didn't feel like power anymore. Lucas saw it for what it was: a never-ending circle that went nowhere. Like those sad mice with the pink eyes in Ms. Elmer's room, the teacher he was glad he didn't have because those mice freaked him out so much. He was like one of those mice, running on a wheel, believing if they just kept going and ran faster, maybe it would take them to a new place, a place they could be free.

He dropped out of the race.

BIG BROTHER

"Look before you leap" was another useful quote. Standing at the edge of the forest and chewing on Dots, Josh wished he'd remembered that particular poster before embarking on the whole running-away-from-school thing.

"Yeah, but 'No use crying over spilled milk,'" the voice buzzed in his ear. Also a poster quote and good advice. But the problem was the voice.

"And," the voice went on, "'Never put off until tomorrow what you can do today.'"

Josh shoved the rest of the Dots in his mouth and started walking. What else could he do? That voice!

The mushed-up, rubbery Dots seemed to expand as he chewed, and his stiff jeans rubbed against his thighs. He tried to swallow, but the Dots glob kept growing. And his jeans—they were doing that thing again. *Run, Josh*, they whispered. *Run.*

"You know," the voice said, "if you wash those jeans like a hundred times, they'll loosen up. You can also buy jeans that are already worn in. I don't know where Mom got those, but, Little Brother, you need some new clothes. Let's go shopping."

That was it. Josh started to run.

The dirt path along the side of the road was uneven and bumpy, with a narrow edge that sloped down to a deep ditch. Evergreen trees crowded the road on either side, so tall they blocked most of the daylight. When the wind caught their pointy tops, they swayed back and forth, like they were laughing. Josh reminded himself that trees were trees. They didn't laugh at people. They weren't about to reach down and snatch him up. Still, he watched them warily until his foot hit a large rock. He stumbled and teetered on the edge of the ditch.

"Whoa, careful," the voice said.

Josh regained his balance and continued on, but by then his breath was wheezy. When he tried to suck in air, the gob of fruit-flavored goo got caught in his throat.

"Gah!" he coughed. "Gah!"

He bent over and heaved up the mess, right into the ditch. Some of his breakfast came up, too: bits of chewed-up cornflakes. He stared at his shoes with their colorful splatter of Dots and cornflakes. Another set of shoes was next to his, also with bits of chewed-up mess. And those shoes—those bigger shoes standing there patiently even with puke on them, well—they were comforting. Like everything about Big Brother had always been.

The heaving ended, but Josh still struggled to catch his breath. He reached around and grabbed his inhaler from the easy-access pocket of his new backpack. When he felt steady, he straightened up and glanced over. Big Brother smiled sympathetically. "You okay?"

Josh wiped his mouth with the back of his hand. He started to walk, and Big Brother fell in step beside him. "Would you like me to go away?"

"Yes," Josh said.

But they both knew what that meant. Because *yes* was a word and with that word he had let him in. He had let him rise from the dirt grave of his old backyard and travel halfway across the country, to this new and unfamiliar place.

Shoulder to shoulder, they continued their walk along the dark forest road. Josh stared at his feet, counting breaths. Finally, when he couldn't stand staring at the half-digested cornflakes anymore, he stopped and rubbed his shoes across a thick patch of grass. Big Brother did the same. "Sorry," Josh said.

Big Brother said, "Who taught you to chew your food?" Which seemed like the funniest thing Josh had ever heard. He laughed so hard his stomach hurt again. "Easy," Big Brother said.

Josh took a deep breath and felt better. He had so much to say. So much to ask. "Well," he said finally.

"Well," said Big Brother. And they smiled, right into each other's eyes.

"Do you still like Lego?" Josh pictured the elaborate colorful cities they used to build together. How they once covered the entire basement floor with a fantastic Lego world. He wanted to be back there again.

"Sure," Big Brother said. "I still like Legos."

"Remember?" Josh asked.

"What?"

"Everything?"

"Of course," he said.

The pine trees were still tall and dark and waving, but Josh didn't feel afraid. He glanced over, waiting for Big Brother to disappear. But he didn't. He seemed as real and solid as anything on the planet. And Josh thought they sort of looked alike, except for the actual muscles and better hair. He was cool, Josh realized, like a Big Brother should be. And seeing him, all grown up like that, made Josh feel something else. Maybe he could be like that, too, someday. Except for the hair.

Big Brother said, "You're pretty fast now."

"Really?" Josh shook his arms, like runners do before a big race. "I've been trying to bend my knees more." He did a little warm-up jog, feeling good. Loose. Hopeful.

"I can tell. You're a superstar."

"Yeah?"

"Absolutely."

Josh thought about asking him to race, like they used to on the far edge of the playground. But that made him remember the awful years of him being gone.

He thought back to the burial ceremony in the backyard. How he'd painted a smooth rock with his name. How they made him dig a hole and put the rock in it. How he was sobbing because he felt they were all burying him alive. But they made him do it anyway, like how other kids did, only with security blankets and binkies.

Josh tried to explain. "They all said I was too old to be playing with an imaginary brother. I mean, that's what they called you—"

"I know."

"Plus the kids at school—"

Big Brother held up his hand. "I know. I was there. I never blamed you."

Josh nodded. "You were gone so long," he said finally. "And now you're all grown up."

"So are you."

"Yeah," Josh said, "except maybe this is all a dream." He pointed to a strange mushroom-like thing growing on the side of a thick pine tree. "Maybe we're a dream of that thing."

"Do you want it to be? A dream of a fungus?" When Josh didn't answer he said, "Do you want me to go away?"

Josh said, "No."

The road was quiet, so quiet that, even from a long way off, Josh heard a car coming. Without thinking, he hopped down into the gulch to hide. Big Brother hopped down too and crouched beside him. It was like one of the games they used to play all the time: Army Patrol, Catch the Robber, Supersecret Spy. It felt, well, pretty great.

"Nice place," Big Brother said, after the car had passed and they'd scrambled back onto the side of the road. He motioned to the trees all around. "You're like a pioneer now. A woodsman."

Josh snorted. "Right."

"Seriously, is there anything you like about this place?"

Josh gave it some thought. "Banana slugs," he said finally. "I saw a picture of one before we moved. It looked exactly like a banana. I thought they'd be everywhere, but I haven't seen one yet."

"Keep looking," Big Brother said.

As they neared the beginning of the string of housing developments, the thick forest gave way to the elaborately manicured entrances. They passed Hidden Peaks and Silver Pines. Cougar Ridge would be next, and then Josh's development. His parents had picked it because they liked how kids were riding their bikes when the real estate lady took them around.

"Why do they all have names like this?" Big Brother asked. "They chop a big hole in the forest and then build all these houses and then give them names to make you think you're still in the chunk of forest that's been cut down."

"I know," Josh said, even though he'd never thought of it like that before. "There's even one called Wilderness, just down the road." Real life was closing in on him. Real life meant confessing to his mother and not just about skipping school.

"Here it is." Josh pointed to the sign for Bear Creek, next to a life-size wooden bear. The bear stood upright, front paws in the air. It looked like it had been carved with a chain saw. "Turn right at the bear."

"Is the bear supposed to be greeting us or scaring us away?"

Josh laughed. "Exactly!" He kept laughing and was afraid he wouldn't be able to stop and maybe he'd puke again and maybe Big Brother would go away, which he was supposed to do. But it all made him afraid.

Big Brother stood and waited. Josh couldn't stop laughing. He made a sound that was some sort of cross between a burp and a hiccup. Big Brother said, "You know what? It's going to be okay."

Josh gulped in air and then hiccup-burped again. "No, it's not. Mom is going to kill me."

"She's not."

"Yeah? Well, Dad's going to find more posters. To fix me."

Big Brother laughed. "Listen, you want some brotherly advice? Get Mom to wash your jeans so they don't make that noise."

"Okay."

"I mean it."

Another car was coming. Josh ducked behind the bear. He decided to ask it, the question they'd both been waiting for. "Why are you here? Why did you come back?"

Big Brother shrugged. "You tell me."

"Seeing you—" Josh fought to find the words. "Seeing you, is pretty much the greatest thing I could hope for. But it makes me wonder. Is there something wrong with me?"

"Nah," Big Brother said easily. "You just have a certain way of seeing the world. You always have."

"Is that bad?"

"It's not bad," he said slowly. "But it's not easy, either." And then he smiled, right into Josh's eyes again. And then he was gone.

Josh spent the rest of the afternoon hiding out in the left-over forest next to Bear Creek. He found a stream with tiny fish and discovered an anthill, swarming with red ants. He searched around trees and poked under leaves looking for banana slugs, but didn't find one. He ate the rest of his candy.

It could have been a bad afternoon, a sad afternoon, a lonely afternoon, but it wasn't. Because Big Brother had found him. From the packed-down dirt in his old backyard to a brand-new school, two time zones away—a school where Josh was supposed to have a fresh start at not being the weird kid—Big Brother had found him.

THE SECOND FIRST DAY

On that Friday tour with Ms. Yoshida, Josh had seen a poster in the locker room. It was a poster of a track star with his arms raised high. The inspirational words, written across the middle, made up the finish-line string he was about to break: *Be the hero of your own story*. Josh thought of his dad when he saw it.

Josh's dad, he loved posters. For birthdays and holidays and just-because days, he would present them to Josh like he was handing off the keys to the kingdom or the secret for getting out of quicksand someday. Back when Josh first learned about the move and had started to cry, his dad said, "Son, what doesn't kill you makes you stronger." And the next day, like magic (only the bad kind), a poster with those exact words appeared in Josh's room.

As Josh got dressed for the second first day of his new school he thought about it, the kill-versus-stronger thing. How could a person ever know which it was going to be? Kill or make stronger? The poster didn't explain that, and neither did his dad.

Even though they were sort of stupid looking, Josh put on his old school uniform khaki pants. Then he grabbed the jeans from the day before, along with all the brand-new jeans folded neatly in his drawer. He took them downstairs where his mom was standing in the kitchen, surrounded by boxes, waiting for Mr. Coffee to stop sputtering.

"Hey, Mom." Josh piled the jeans on top of a box labeled POTS & PANS. "Could you maybe wash these for me?"

"Did you get them all dirty already?"

"No. They're just hard to walk in. They make a noise."

"Okay," she said. "Sure, honey." She handed him a bowl of cornflakes. Josh tried not to think about how they had looked the day before, halfway digested and splattered across his shoes.

"So about yesterday. I feel like I didn't do enough to prepare you for success."

He knew she was trying to make him feel better about running away from his first day of school, but it made him feel worse. He avoided her eyes by studying the yellow flakes swimming in milk. "It wasn't that, Mom. I just didn't want to walk in late."

"That's what I mean. Today is a new start, Josh, and we don't want you to get into some of those old patterns. Ms. Yoshida is going to meet you at drop-off and get you to class—"

"Mom, no!"

She held up her hand. "And if you need help, you know what to do."

Like the morning before, Josh's mother dropped him off in the parking lot. Only this time there was no rash scratching or long goodbye because Ms. Yoshida was waiting on the curb. He opened his mouth to tell her the truth about the day before—that Big Brother had returned—and then he closed it. He couldn't tell her, not until he had successfully completed a real first day. He would wait until after school, when he could share the bad news with good.

"Don't forget this." She handed him the red raincoat.

"Mom—"

"It's supposed to rain later. Unless you want me to pick you up after school?"

Josh shook his head. He grabbed the coat and stepped out of the car. Ms. Yoshida's smile was extra bright. She waved to Josh's mom and then led Josh to his classroom in building C, where the teacher, Mr. K, made a big deal of introducing him to the class. Mr. K talked about community and being new to a school. He asked Josh all the standard questions about Chicago. Josh said, "It's colder in winter. And hotter in summer." Some of the kids laughed.

Mr. K was nice, but he made Josh remember Mr. Lombardi, from kindergarten. How sometimes, even the nicest grown-ups didn't know that there were different rules for kids.

Still, it was all easier than Josh thought it would be. His pants didn't mock him. His nose didn't itch so there was no danger of Kleenex. Except for the initial introductions, no one paid much attention to him at all.

THE ROPES

Lucas had been hunched over his desk, doodling on his brainstorm sheet, but when the new kid walked into the classroom, his body automatically straightened—like the ears of a dog when it picks up a sound no one else can hear. Lucas quickly added that—*dogs' ears*—to his Marvelous Mysteries brainstorm sheet. Then he turned back to the boy.

The boy wasn't wearing the red raincoat, although upon closer inspection, Lucas did see that he was holding it in his hand, so low that it dragged on the floor. Anyway, Lucas would have recognized him without it. There was something about him.

Mr. K was trying to be nice, but Lucas felt bad for the lump of a kid standing there, clinging to his red raincoat. His eyes darted around the room, like he was hoping to find a magic portal instead of an empty seat.

Mr. K was making small talk and jokes about the rain.

When he asked the new kid about Chicago, no one could hear what he said. Something about cold. Or maybe he said hot? Then Mr. K told the new kid to pick a seat, any seat, and try not to sit in the same seat the next day.

"Isthatarule?" the kid mumbled.

"Excuse me?"

"Isthatarule?" he tried again. Someone laughed and the kid basically turned to petrified wood.

"Is it a rule?" Mr. K finally managed to decipher. "No. It's not a rule but a policy. It gives you the chance to see the world in a different way, every day. Right class?"

"Right, Mr. K!"

The boy mumbled something else and waited, but Mr. K looked confused again so the boy just shuffled down the closest aisle, looking for a seat. Everyone used that as an excuse to start talking.

Mr. K clap-clapped. "Ready-set?"

Clap-clap. "You-bet!" the class answered.

"Okay, who would like to volunteer to be Josh Duncan's buddy? To show him the ropes this week?"

Lucas thought about raising his hand, but he didn't really know what the ropes were and he didn't want to look stupid. He was considering anyway, just because Josh Duncan looked so sad, but Liddy Franklin, who volunteered for everything, already had her hand in the air.

"Thank you, Liddy. I know you'll do a great job of showing Josh around and making him feel welcome here and . . ."

Mr. K was still speaking, but something happened that made Lucas forget all about the rope talk. It was the shadow—the weird shadow he'd seen the day before, when the boy was running past the window. It was there again. Following Josh Duncan.

Wait, no. That wasn't completely accurate. Lucas didn't see it as much as he felt it. But could a person feel a shadow? Could a shadow move on its own, away from the person it's supposed to be attached to?

Even though Mr. K said there was no such thing as a stupid question, Lucas believed some questions really were sort of stupid. Like the shadow questions. He studied yesterday's entry on his brainstorm sheet: *Shadows on a day with no sun.*

When he glanced back, Josh Duncan was dropping his pencil and stepping on his coat and making an all-around disaster of trying to sit down. Lucas no longer saw a shadow, but he did see Maxie Moon.

Maxie was watching the new kid with a keen interest, like a cat, maybe, staring at a mouse. For the first time, Lucas had the terrible realization: Maxie Moon might hang around for the rest of his life. Or at least until she got what she wanted from him.

He wrote, *What does she want from me?*

"People!" Mr. K had the Marvelous Mysteries presentation schedule sheet out and was waving it in the air. "People! What's going on? No one has signed up. We need to get this ball rolling! How about a volunteer for tomorrow?" He peered over the glasses sliding down his nose. Somehow, miraculously, he didn't look silly.

Lucas added, *Why do some people look funny with their glasses sliding off their noses, but others don't?*

"Scholars! Scientists! I need a volunteer!"

This was one of those times when no one made eye contact with the teacher. How did they all know to do that, as a group? Was it an understanding people were born with? Was it from the animal kingdom? Lucas picked up his pencil again and sighed as he added it to his brainstorm sheet. He was starting to think that everything in the world was a Marvelous Mystery.

He snuck a quick glance at Mr. K, not long enough to make eye contact, but long enough to see why he was being so quiet. Mr. K was just perched there on the edge of his desk, with his silly-not-silly glasses. Lucas wanted to raise his hand and say, "Mr. K, your glasses might fall off the end of your nose if you don't push them back," but he was afraid Mr. K would think he was volunteering to go first. How could he go first? He wasn't even done brainstorming!

Liddy Franklin stuck her arm in the air again. Mr. K clapped enthusiastically. "Liddy! Wonderful—"

"No, Mr. K." She waved her hands in a panic. "I'm not volunteering. I have a question."

"Okay, Liddy. What's your question?"

"It's just that we've never done anything like this before. And you didn't really give us any direction or worksheet—"

"You have a topic brainstorm sheet."

"I know. But I mean, there's no outline. You know, for our presentations. Like, it can really be anything? Because whenever I ask you what the presentation should be like, or how long, or if we should make a poster or bring in props, or like do a PowerPoint or something, you never answer."

Heads around the classroom nodded. Vigorously.

The moment she said it—and as much as Lucas didn't want to agree with anything Liddy Franklin ever said—he knew it was exactly what he was feeling. And why he just kept adding to his list instead of starting his project. No one had shown him how to put together a project with no outline or rules or assigned topic.

Mr. K swept his eyes across the room. "Liddy," he said. "It looks like you've spoken for the class."

More heads nodded.

"And you are right. But I've deliberately kept this project open because I want you to let your topic be your guide. You can do anything. Really. Anything. Anything that seems like it best represents the Marvelous Mystery you are trying to share. Does that make sense?"

Heads froze.

Mr. K let out a long, low whistle, then startled them all when he jumped up suddenly. His glasses fell off his nose and clattered on the floor, but he didn't pick them up. "Okay, how about this. How about I go first? I'll take the first slot tomorrow. Would that help?"

Everyone said it would, yes, for certain, that would be great.

"But remember, what I do is not what you will do. In fact, if everyone ends up following my lead, then this won't work."

"We'll get a bad grade?" Liddy again. But it could have been anyone.

"How about—" Mr. K paused for a moment, to pick up his glasses. "How about just this once we don't worry about grades? How about we dive into our mysteries with open minds, ready for discovery? Ready to share what we find in whatever way makes the most sense for our findings? How about that?" He perched his glasses back on the bridge of his nose and beamed out at the class, but everyone was suddenly busy looking down at their desks again.

Lucas wrote, *Eye contact.*

Then, because he couldn't help it, he snuck a glance at the

back corner seat. Maxie Moon had turned all her attention on Mr. K. Her eyes were shining and for a moment, just one moment, a deep feeling of sorrow swept over Lucas. A wave of sorrow and a flash of memory for the girl she'd once been, the friend she'd once been.

His best friend.

If a Marvelous Mystery project could answer the question of Maxie Moon, then his brainstorming would be over. That's the one he would choose. But he knew it was impossible. Maxie Moon was a different kind of mystery. A secret mystery. A tragic mistake. The kind that kept him looking the other way.

DEAD MELANIE

"Next!" the cafeteria lady shouted. Josh stepped up to the counter with his lunch card.

"You want two slices?"

He nodded.

"Pepperoni?"

Even though he wanted plain cheese, he nodded again, mostly because of how disastrous it had been when he'd tried to talk in Mr. K's class. It was like all the words had been rolled in Elmer's Glue.

She slid two thick slices of pepperoni pizza onto a paper plate and set the plate on an orange tray. "Here you go." She was wearing a hairnet, like Josh's cafeteria lady back home.

"Thank you." The words came out sort of normal sounding so Josh added, "This is my first day."

She smiled. "Welcome. You'll love it here."

"Really?"

"Of course. These are the happiest years of your life."

"Oh, good," Josh said. "Thank you." He turned and faced the cafeteria. All the tables were full, with even more kids pushing through the doors. He saw Liddy, the girl who was supposed to show him the ropes, but she was already at a table with a bunch of friends. Somehow, as soon as the bell rang, she'd abandoned the rope thing.

Josh didn't mind too much. Except that the cafeteria had always been his least favorite place. Rules existed, but not ones that he could totally understand. And there were just too many things coming at him: eyebrows and braces and laughter and backpacks and the mixed-together smell of sour milk and green beans and tater tots. Josh saw nothing and he saw it all. His legs stopped working. Elbows and earrings and some of the eighth graders were as big as grown-ups and was that a mustache even? His heart pounded. Someone was quacking like a duck. He hoped it wasn't him.

At his old school he'd eat lunch in a classroom with one of the nice teachers who would let kids do that. Sometimes, when the teachers were in a meeting, he'd sneak into the library, even though no food was allowed. He wished he'd planned ahead for this moment, this terrible moment with lunch tray in hand and bodies all around.

Mind racing, he considered the media center, but it was too new and wide-open. What about the old library—the alien-ship building above the Hello Walk? The sign said DO NOT ENTER, but was the door actually locked? And just how haunted was it?

Someone bumped his shoulder, turning him sideways. He spotted Ms. Yoshida at the far end of the cafeteria and almost dropped his tray. A voice in his ear whispered, "Ditch the tray."

Josh spun around. Big Brother!

"Ditch the tray and follow me."

"Ditch the—" he started, but Big Brother put his finger to his lips and pointed to the orange tray. "Just bring your plate."

Josh set the tray on top of a nearby garbage can. He followed Big Brother out the door, back toward the main buildings, and around the perimeter of the Hello Walk. There, in a forgotten-looking corner hidden by bushes, was a bench.

"It looked like you needed a moment," Big Brother said. "To catch your breath."

"You're right." Josh thought back to the first day, the very first day. The Kleenex day. Big Brother had saved him then, too.

On the backrest of the bench was an engraved plaque with

swirly letters. Josh bent closer to read: MELANIE PRICE—WE WILL NEVER FORGET.

"Never forget what—" he started. And then, "Hey! This is a dead girl's bench!"

"So?"

"So it's creepy. Don't I have enough creepy in my life?"

Big Brother snorted. He sat down and leaned his back against the swirly letters that spelled out a dead girl's name. "You can always go back to the cafeteria."

Josh stared at the bench, then down at his lunch. Grease was seeping into the paper plate, circling the pizza like a moat. A fat, slow bumblebee, probably left over from summer, lumbered next to his foot.

Big Brother said, "Eat up."

"How do you think she died?"

"Seriously, sit down."

Josh sat, and the cement bench was cold through the cotton khakis of his old school uniform pants. "Do you think she's buried here?"

"What? No! It's just a bench. They put it here so her friends will remember her."

Josh picked off the thin slices of pepperoni and stacked them on the side of the plate.

"You okay?" Big Brother asked.

Josh nodded. Things hadn't been that bad. They'd been surprisingly pretty easy. But it was just so much to take in. "It's not like I expected to make a bunch of friends right away," he said. "But—" He shook his head. "Everything is fine. No one teased me, or called me a name."

"Not really a poster quote."

Josh shrugged.

"What about friends?"

Josh pulled out his notebook and opened it to a page with names from his class, including relevant details that might be useful as conversation starters. He said, "There are prospects."

Big Brother stared at the notebook. "It's easy for some people. It's hard for others." He said it in a nice way, which is sometimes harder to hear than a mean way. It made Josh embarrassed about his notebook, and how he'd written out the names with such hopeful penmanship.

Why, Josh wanted to ask. Why was it so hard? Because really. No one had ever explained that and Josh really wanted to know.

Big Brother said slowly, "I think it will get easier, when you get older. I think you'll find your way and meet people who see the world a little differently, too. You're a good kid. You're kind and smart. You're brave."

"I am?"

"Sure. Like how you showed up today? Brave."

Josh said, "Going to school is just normal stuff."

"Normal stuff requires bravery, for some people more than others. You could do that for your Marvelous Mystery project. Bravery."

Josh shook his head. "It's not that kind of project."

"It can be anything you want."

Josh was annoyed. The Big Brother he remembered was for playing at recess and building Lego cities. Not for being a homework boss. What did he know, anyway? It was easy for him, with his new big biceps and excellent hair. What did he know about the real world? Josh closed his notebook.

"You have grease on your chin. Don't you have a napkin?"

Josh wiped his face with the back of his hand. "You sound like Mom. And anyway, no one has even noticed me. Even my rope person forgot about me the minute the bell rang."

"Yeah, but walk around with grease on your chin like that. And keep talking to yourself. Then they will. They'll notice you."

"You know what? You know what?" He was this close to crying, so he closed his eyes. "I'm not talking to myself. I'm talking to you. And I'm only talking to you because you showed up."

When Josh opened his eyes, Big Brother was gone. "Good

riddance," he muttered, and even as it came out of his mouth he realized it was something an eighty-year-old woman would say, which was probably part of the problem, at least socially, but—good riddance anyway!

Josh opened his notebook and ripped out the pages with his name chart and notes. He grabbed his pizza plate and dumped the whole mess of grease and goo and relevant information into the trash. Good riddance, he thought again.

The first bell rang, but Josh stayed where he was, halfway hiding behind the garbage can and a large green rhododendron bush. Which is where he was when he saw her, for the very first time.

She was at the edge of the Hello Walk, standing alone but near a group of kids. Josh recognized a few of them from Mr. K's class, but couldn't remember any names. He wished he had his name chart, but it was in the trash.

"See?" he whispered. "Relevant."

Maybe the girl stood out to him because her shoes were two different colors, or because her shirt had a sparkly rainbow. Or maybe it was just the strange way she hovered there, on the edge of everything.

Or maybe it was because of the twitch.

Sometimes bodies know before brains do. Bodies will send prickles on the back of a neck, or goose bumps up and down an arm. As Josh moved closer to peer through the bushy green leaves of the plant, he felt that shift in his body. His hands got clammy and his neck began to twitch.

SOS, his neck said.

And when she turned to look straight at him, he knew. It wasn't just Big Brother anymore. The crack was wide-open.

THE CRACK

They used to show up everywhere, at the park and at school. At the grocery store while Josh trailed behind his mom in the frozen food aisle. He pictured a crack in the universe, one that Big Brother had made on that first day of kindergarten. Once the crack was there, the rest of them had spilled out, like insects from a rotting log.

It was always the same. First, they would stand at a distance, blinking in a surprised way. Then, when they spotted Josh watching, they would approach slowly, eyes shifting sideways, like stray dogs will sometimes do. Josh, not knowing any better, would always be friendly and welcoming. "Hello," he'd say. "Come to my house."

Because they were fun. They wanted to play.

Well, most of them. Some took a quick look around and slipped right back from where they came. Some hung out for a while and then were gone. The kids stayed the longest—they played on the monkey bars and came home for dinner. Had pillow fights in Josh's room at night.

Oh, and there was a pirate captain. He shadowed Josh on the playground for a few weeks. Then one day, when Josh was stuck in the middle of the monkey bars, he limped up on his wooden leg and growled, "Well, well, well." That's all he ever said. Well, well, well. But they had fun playing together. He liked Josh's Tinkertoys.

His parents: They read some books that said imaginary friends were normal, blah-blah-blah. So for a long time they let Josh play with his old friends and kid friends and pirate captain. Then, on his eighth birthday, he invited his entire class to his house for a party. Actually, his parents invited them. And no one came. But Josh had a good time anyway because his real friends slipped through and showed up, each and every one of them.

They played hide-and-seek. They built a pillow fort. They sang "Happy Birthday" in seven different languages and helped Josh blow out the candles. They ate as much cake as they wanted. Everyone got along, even the pirate captain.

Josh's parents were worried and set him up with Dr. Ted, who, they explained, was a "talking doctor." And Dr. Ted talked. And the problem was solved. Except for Big Brother. He was the one friend Josh couldn't let go.

So his parents had him dig a hole in the backyard. And in it went all his baby things, including the rock Josh had painted with Big Brother's name. "These things are gone now," his parents said. And the problem went away.

At least, that's how it seemed. But even after Big Brother stopped showing up, the problem of making real friends didn't go away. The problem of being alone didn't go away. The problem of being different didn't go away.

On his second first day of school, as Josh made his way past the line of buses in the parking lot, he practiced how he would tell his mom about everything. Like Big Brother and the sparkling girl. Because he knew he was supposed to. Would she ever be able to see it the way he did? The invisible crack? Or was it something that was impossible to believe unless you'd seen it with your own eyes, starting at the age of five?

He knew the answer, of course, and his situation made him think about that poster that his dad had, with a kitten surrounded by rocks and a puppy: *Stuck between a rock and a hard place.*

It was supposed to be funny, the poster. Sometimes his dad just got funny posters. Like the other kitten one, where the kitten is clinging to a tree branch with the words, *Hang in there.* But both posters just made Josh sad. He was the kitten who was trying to hang in there. He was also stuck between a rock and a hard place.

Josh passed bus #39 and kept going. When his parents had registered him at Mountain View K–8, he'd been given the option of taking that bus or walking home. He chose walking. "Even in the rain?" his mom had asked. And he'd nodded. The thing he hated most at his old school was stumbling down the bus aisle, looking for a seat.

"Excuse me, can I sit here?"

But now, as he squared his backpack on his shoulders and headed for the main road, Josh wasn't so sure about his decision. He was tired and hungry. When he thought about the pizza he'd thrown away at lunch, his stomach made an angry rumble.

Josh tried to conjure an inspirational phrase that would help him get home. Which poster quote would his dad use? The only one he could think of was "When life gives you lemons, make lemonade." Which did not work. Josh was pretty sure that one would never work. Not for anything.

Town was the same as the day before with its sidewalks and stores and people. And at the edge of town The Last Stop still advertised corn dogs, two for one, right next to the price of gasoline. Josh would have liked a corn dog. Or two. His stomach rumbled again. But he'd spent all his allowance on candy.

Since the walk the day before had been filled with the surprising return of Big Brother and the dramatic upchucking of cornflakes and Dots, Josh hadn't noticed how alone he was out there on the road next to the forest. How dark and creepy and cold it was. He thought about the names of the housing developments: Cougar Ridge and Bear Creek. Wilderness. Did they get their names from real cougars and bears? True wilderness?

A branch snapped, just on the other side of the ditch. Josh started to run. All the sounds in the forest—the creepy, mysterious, twig-snapping animal sounds—seemed to run alongside him, matching his pace. His backpack pounded against his shoulder blades, his breath got wheezy, and his red raincoat made him sweat, but Josh didn't slow down, not even when he almost tripped over an old mailbox post that was rotting on the ground.

When he heard the rumble of a motor coming up from behind Josh wondered if he should jump into the ditch again, to hide. But he wasn't doing anything wrong. He wasn't skipping school like the day before. He was just walking home. Like kids did. So he straightened his shoulders and looked straight ahead.

The vehicle lumbered past with a blast of smoky air. It was a bright yellow school bus, #39. Other kids were traveling along the same forest road to their homes. The bus reminded Josh of that. It made him less afraid.

The feeling of safety lasted all the way to the carved sign and wooden bear. "Welcome home," the bear's waving paw seemed to say.

Josh looked the bear straight in the eye, grateful for his calm wooden presence. "Thanks," he said. "See you later."

"Alligator," the bear said with a wink, making Josh laugh out loud.

#39

"You're missing the point!" Maxie Moon's voice was in his ear. Lucas had forgotten that detail about her, back when they were little kids and best friends—how she used to start a conversation in the middle. It was like she always had a conversation going on in her head, and at some point the words would just spill out.

He'd forgotten that about her.

He'd also forgotten that if he didn't respond, she would respond for him. So as he stayed perfectly still, with his forehead pressed against the rattling window of bus #39, Maxie Moon continued.

"The point is, the topic is supposed to be something you want to learn about, more than anything else. *Anything* else. And *you*—what *you* want to learn. Capiche?"

Oh, right. That was another thing. She threw in Italian

words sometimes, like her grandmother from Italy did, who lived with their family.

Used to live with their family.

Lucas closed his eyes. He wanted to tell her to go away, but he'd always been told that if you wanted someone to leave you alone, ignoring was the most effective strategy.

"So maybe," she continued, "your Marvelous Mysteries project could be about me. About us. About how we used to be best friends. What do you think about that? Friendship? What makes people best friends? What makes them stop being best friends? Maybe it goes like this: I once had a best friend. We had the most fun together any friends can have. And then she was gone. How's that for a start?"

The bus lurched to a stop and Lucas opened his eyes. Only two stops left. He shouted, "Bye, Ruby!" and Ruby shouted back, "See you tomorrow."

"So nice," Maxie Moon whispered.

"Hey, Jordon," Lucas called to his buddy who was two seats up. Jordon turned around and grinned. "You going to the Panthers game on Friday?"

"I think so."

"Me too." If he just kept talking to his friends, if he just kept talking and laughing with them, maybe she would finally get the idea. It seemed to work okay, except Jordon was getting off next along with Amir and Frankie. One by one, his friends exited the bus. Wilderness, where he lived, was the very last stop.

Lucas turned back to the window, just in time to see a flash of red. He recognized the boy stumbling along the side of the road. It was Josh Duncan.

"Right there." Maxie Moon was whispering in his ear again. "The mailbox has fallen down and no one will pick it up. But you can see it, if you look close enough. And the road is there. Don't you remember? Maybe that should be your project. The house is a mystery, don't you think? You could go out there again. Just follow the trail through the trees."

That's when Lucas understood what she was saying, and where they were. It was the road into the woods that led to the house. The old Cascalenda house. Maxie Moon's house.

Over the years he'd done his best to ignore it. To push it out of his mind. To not see the fallen mailbox and overgrown drive. Now he jumped to his feet and lurched down the aisle.

The bus driver glanced in his rearview mirror. "Stay seated until the bus comes to a complete stop, please."

Heart pounding, Lucas slid into an empty seat near the front. He wished he could make the bus go faster. What did she want? What did she want from him?

Then he heard her in his ear again, like a buzzing that was there always but he could only tune in sometimes. "I'm here because of you. That's why I'm here. Capiche?"

Lucas knew one thing for certain. Maxie Moon was determined to get something from him. He had no idea what it was, but he did know this: Maxie didn't stop until she got exactly what she wanted.

BOXES

With its wide sidewalks, smooth, winding streets, and manicured lawns, Bear Creek housing development was the opposite sort of creepy from the dark and untamed forest. But it was definitely creepy.

Before the move, when they were still back in Chicago, Josh's parents had pulled up the Bear Creek website and let him choose which color he'd like their new house to be. There were three options: beige, gray, or blue. Josh picked blue. From the photo, it had looked the cheeriest. In person, beige, gray, and blue were pretty much the same. Inside, the walls were a color called taupe. His parents had taken Josh to the hardware store and let him pick out a new color for his bedroom. He chose the exact shade of yellow that his old bedroom walls had been.

Now, the blank taupe walls greeted him at the front door.

"Mom?" he called. No answer. He found her on the floor in the living room, surrounded by cardboard boxes. She glanced up and smiled. "How'd it go today?"

He could tell by the way she asked that she'd already been on the phone with Ms. Yoshida. "Good," he said.

"You had a buddy, right? Someone who showed you around?"

"Yeah. She showed me the ropes." His mom wanted more, he could see it in her eyes. "And I had pizza for lunch."

She nodded. "That's great."

"Yeah."

He stood there, in the echo-chamber house, smelling paint fumes, not knowing what to say next. Finally his mother said, "I came up with a plan."

"A plan?"

"For getting the house in order. I'm going to unpack the kitchen boxes. Then start on the living room. But before I do any of that, I need to clear some space." She motioned to the towering stacks of boxes. "I guess you don't know how much stuff you have until you need to move it all."

Josh knew he should bring up the Big Brother thing, but when he noticed that the rash on the back of her hand was even more red and bumpy, he decided to wait.

She said, "I thought I'd move some of these to the garage for now. Will you help me with that?"

"Sure." Josh reached for a box while his mom sat back on her heels and pushed the hair out of her face. That's when she seemed to notice him for real.

"Why are you jerking your head?"

Josh clamped his hand on his twitching neck. "I'm not."

She leaned forward. "Is everything really okay?"

He stared at her rash. "Everything is great, Mom." As he said it, he came up with a poster idea: "Never tell your mother something today that can wait until tomorrow." He quickly picked up a box and hauled it out to the garage, accidentally kicking over one of the cans of leftover paint, the yellow he'd chosen for his room.

"Mom!" he shouted. "I spilled the paint!" It ended up being a lucky accident because it sent her into panic mode, finding turpentine and old rags, then sopping and scraping and scrubbing the spilled paint. It meant the conversation was over. At least for the moment.

After that they hauled box after box into the garage. Josh worked hard and fast so he wouldn't have to talk. Every once in a while he remembered to say, "Whew!" or "So many boxes!"

Still, he could feel his mother's laser-beam eyes. When she went back into the house to call his dad, Josh said, "Whew!" for real and sat down on a box. Through the closed door he could hear some of what she said.

He heard: *Neck.*

And: *Twitch.*

And: *Worried.*

"Wow." Big Brother stepped out from behind a pile of cardboard. "When did she get like that?"

"She's always this way about me now. Always looking for a sign. Ever since, you know. Ever since *you.*" Josh tried to hide how happy he was to see him.

Big Brother nodded solemnly. "I feel personally responsible."

Josh laughed. No matter how dire the situation, Big Brother could always make him laugh. Then he stopped laughing and stared at his shoes. "I thought you might have gone away again. When I was walking home today and it was creepy by the woods and you didn't come."

"But you made it home okay, didn't you? You were brave."

Josh shrugged. He hadn't felt brave. He said, "I almost told her about you."

"Why didn't you?"

Josh didn't know how to answer. He didn't understand it himself. He thought about the girl with the shoes and sparkly shirt. How could he put words around something there weren't really words for? And what if he did find the right words? Did that mean Big Brother would go away again? Forever this time? What would the world look like then?

The phone conversation was still going on in the other room, and he could hear the high pitch of his mother's voice.

"Listen," Big Brother said quickly. "You need to make some changes around here. That's what the move was all about, right?"

"We moved for Dad's job."

"Right, but it's also for you. To start over. To make friends. Don't forget—I'm here to help you. Like a big brother is supposed to."

Josh pushed at boxes. "Then help me find the Lego," he said.

"I'm not here to play with Legos."

"First of all, they are just called Lego. Not Legos. Second of all, you don't actually *play* with Lego. You create worlds." Josh hated the way his voice sounded right then—like a cranky five-year-old—but he couldn't stop. "What? You think you're too old for Lego? You think I'm too old for Lego? Is that what this is about?"

"No one is ever too old for Legos," Big Brother said calmly. "But you are facing some monumental challenges with this move. And Dad's not home to share his inspiring poster quotes—"

Josh couldn't help it. He laughed again.

"And Mom does not have a clue about the social realities of a new school. So that leaves me, Big Brother. We'll play with Legos after we find your bike."

"My bike? My *bike*?" Josh didn't laugh this time. "You

know I don't ride my bike. Not since that last time. I don't think we even brought it. Remember when those jerks chased me? Remember that dog?"

"Find your bike," he said. "Or else—"

"Or else what?"

"Joshua Duncan!"

Josh spun around to see his mom in the doorway, arms folded over her chest and hair pulled back in a tight new ponytail. "Who are you talking to?" She narrowed her eyes into extreme laser-beam mode.

"I think you're supposed to say 'whom.'"

"Well, then. Whom are you talking to?"

"That sounds weird, though, doesn't it? Maybe, 'to whom are you talking—'"

"Josh." She took a step closer.

"I was just looking for . . . I was looking for my bike."

"But you were talking. I heard you."

(Don't even talk to yourself!)

"I wasn't talking, Mom. I might have been singing. I don't know. Honestly, I was just looking for my bike."

What followed was a monumental stare-down. "Do not look away," Big Brother whispered in Josh's ear. "Even though her eyes are so freaky right now."

His eyes started to water, but Josh stayed still and forced them not to blink. Finally his mom broke her stare. She muttered, "We need some fresh air in here," and pushed the garage door button. As the door rumbled open, she said, "Those paint fumes are not good for your lungs."

"I'm sorry."

She mumbled something more about the mess, how turpentine was toxic, and the rags were a fire hazard.

"Mom, I said I'm sorry. I didn't mean to kick over—"

"You never ride your bike." It came out like an accusation.

"Yeah, but now I will. All the kids do. Isn't that why we moved here? So I would ride my bike and stuff?"

"What about a helmet? You are not riding a bike without a helmet."

"I have one somewhere." Josh turned and faced the boxes, all labeled with thick black marker: LIVING ROOM, DINING ROOM, KITCHEN, FRAGILES, BABY. He froze, holding on to BABY.

"What's the matter?" Big Brother, in his ear.

Josh's head felt dizzy. He was still touching the box with the baby stuff. For a moment his hand tingled.

"Oh yeah," Big Brother whispered. "Sad. Now find your helmet."

Josh pushed the box aside and busied himself with the next stack until he found the one he was looking for: JOSH SPORT.

Ripping it open, he dug past unused roller blades and shin guards and baseball gloves until he found it, at the very bottom. He yanked it out and set it on his head. "See?" he said.

The helmet might have fit okay when Josh was six or seven, but now he had to pull hard at the straps to be able to pinch them together under his chin. He managed to move his mouth just enough to say, "So do you know where my bike is?"

His mom shrugged and turned away, but not before Josh saw her eyes shift to the far dark corner. He went right over. Hidden behind a stack of rakes and shovels was his bike, smaller than he remembered. Still, he pulled it out and dragged it to the driveway.

"Josh! You will absolutely kill yourself!"

Josh knew she was probably right, but it was hard to think logically with his brain squished by his tiny helmet. Swinging his leg over the seat, he tried to make his voice sound calm. "What does Dad always say? There are two things you have to do in life: pay taxes and ride a bike."

"But it's so small! It's too small for you, Josh."

Josh's knees banged against the handlebars when he tried to pedal. He wobbled and tipped and almost fell. But then something changed. It was as if suddenly, two strong hands were holding him up. And from somewhere far away, a crowd started to cheer. Those hands and that cheering, they made his legs pump faster, which, after all, is the key to staying upright on a bike.

Josh's mom stood at the end of the driveway, scratching her rash. "Be careful!" she called.

Josh was surprised by how good it felt to be out on a bike. Actually, how great it felt. He followed the curvy street until he came to a stop. He took a right, then a left. He traveled farther out and in a different direction than he had before with his mom.

When he turned around and started back, all the streets and houses looked like his. But one street had a bunch of little kids, all on bikes. They were zooming in circles and popping wheelies. Their bikes were pretty much the same size, but Josh didn't care.

"You're doing great," Big Brother said in his ear.

"Thanks. It was all your idea."

"The first of many," he said. "And it's death and taxes."

"What?"

"The two things you can't escape. According to Dad."

"Oh. What's the one about riding your bike?"

"You never forget how to ride a bike."

Josh said, "Well, that's surprisingly true. Dad's right about that."

He thought about his dad, how happy he'd be at that moment. He always wanted Josh to be out in the neighborhood, a member of the army of kids on bikes. And as Josh turned another corner he finally understood why: It felt good to be moving smooth and fast because of his own two legs. It felt like freedom.

Big Brother said, "Fun, huh? Now you need to get Mom to let you ride your bike to school."

"Yeah, right."

"I mean it."

"But Mom drives me in the morning. And I walk home. That's the deal."

"That's going to change."

"Why?"

"Because I said so."

Josh's neck twitched. "It's too small for me. And it's bright yellow. With SpongeBob all over it."

"You can raise the seat, you know. And the handlebars. You just need a wrench. It's fairly straightforward. And you should adjust the straps on your helmet—"

"Why are you being so bossy?"

"Because I have plans for you," he said softly. "That's why I'm here."

"You can't just come back and make plans."

"If you want me to stay," he said, "that's how it's going to be."

Josh turned his SpongeBob bicycle in a wide, wobbly circle and rode away from Big Brother. A crow called down from a wire, like it had some important news to report.

Josh heard Big Brother. "Life is a glorious adventure."

"What?" he snapped back over his shoulder. "What are you yakking about now?"

"Today," he called. "When you were searching for an inspirational quote before your walk home. Here's one: 'Life is a glorious adventure . . . or it is nothing.'"

Josh put down his head and pedaled furiously away.

SKELETON HOUSES

Josh had been in such a hurry to get away from Big Brother's bossy voice that he hadn't paid much attention to where he was riding. After a series of wrong turns he found himself at the far edge of the development, right next to the forest. Rising above a mess of dirt piles, tree stumps, and rough, trampled grass were several new Bear Creek homes, under construction. Josh stopped and straddled his bike. He had seen houses being built, but he'd never examined one closely. Houses have bones, he thought. Wooden bones.

He looked past the gaping skeleton houses to the thick dark forest. The air had gone still, as if the birds and insects and even the wind were waiting for something in that strange borderland between civilization and forest.

Josh knew that this would all be put together. There would be plywood and trim and thick coats of paint to cover everything. All the ratty dirt patches would be smoothed, and chunks of green lawn would be rolled out to make yards. Then the street would get a name. Buttercup Lane, maybe, or Chestnut Way. And people would drive up with their boxes of stuff and never think about what had come before. But for now there was this: the in-between space that had not been completely tamed.

The sun dropped low to the circle of trees and a new chill crept into the air. Josh shivered and turned his bike around. He tried not to think ahead, to the ride back through the maze of streets that all looked the same. He wished Big Brother would show up and help him find his way.

He heard noises then—shouting and laughter—and found himself being overtaken by a group of kids on bikes. They were the same kids he'd passed earlier, four of them, riding up fast.

Josh's heart pounded. He judged they were in second grade, maybe third. Their bikes seemed threatening, with thick tires and fire-patterned racing stripes. When they circled around, Josh saw they were carrying objects—boards and bricks and chunks of cement. One kid had a bright-orange traffic cone. For a moment, no one spoke. Then a crow called from a nearby tree, breaking the silence.

"Hello," one of the kids said.

"Hello," said Josh.

"You want to jump with us?"

"Jump?"

"We're going to make an obstacle course."

"Oh," Josh said. "Thanks, but I have to go home."

The kids nodded and rode ahead to the dirt mound behind the skeleton house. Josh really did need to be going home but he stayed where he was, watching as the four kids turned the building site into something else: an obstacle course with ramps and jumps and cones. When it was finished, they lined up at the far edge of the dirt yard and took turns. They cheered when one of them landed the perfect jump and ran over to check when another fell.

"Loser touches the house!" they called, over and over.

One girl left her bike in the dirt after a wipeout. She walked over to Josh with a slight limp. "I thought you said you had to go home."

"Well, I do." He cleared his throat. "Are you okay?"

She nodded and bent over to brush off her jeans. "You should try it."

He shook his head.

"Why are you just standing here?"

Josh didn't actually know why he was. Just standing there. He looked at the construction site that was now a track. "I'm new here. I was just . . . riding around." It was the only thing he could think to say.

"I like your bike."

"Thanks." Josh was embarrassed but also pleased. She asked what grade he was in and he told her. Then she told him that she was in second grade, at Mountain View K–8. "That's where I go, too," he said. "But I just started."

Two other kids dropped their bikes and ran over. "He's just standing here," the girl informed them.

One of the boys had a sling on his arm. "You're brave. We never come here alone."

"Yeah," another added.

Josh felt his face flush. "I'm not brave."

The girl said, "He's new. He doesn't know."

"Know what?"

One of the kids pointed. "See that path over there? The one that goes into the forest? If you walk on that path, you come to an old house where somebody died. A girl. It's all boarded up but there are noises that come from the walls. Like crying and stuff."

"Nobody can live there," another one said.

Josh squinted to where the boy was pointing. He saw a tall pine tree, covered with dark shapes. Crows. There must have been fifty of them!

The kids saw him looking. "Do you know what a group of crows is called?"

Josh thought. "A flock?"

"No. A murder."

"That can't be right."

"It is. And the crows get mad if we look at them. They can recognize faces."

Josh turned his face, so the crows wouldn't be able to recognize it. "Have you gone in there?" Josh asked. "On the trail?"

"It's no trespassing."

"Then how do you know about the house?"

The four zipped their mouths tight and glanced sideways at each other. The first girl said quickly, "Why don't you want to try our obstacle course? It's fun. Loser touches the house. But we won't make you do it."

"What does that mean?" Josh asked.

"Whoever wipes out the most has to sneak into the woods and touch the house." The other three glared at the girl, whose mouth had obviously come unzipped. She shrugged them off like it didn't matter. "He's not going to tell anybody."

"I won't," Josh said. "Tell anybody. But I can't ride your obstacle course. I have to go home now." Still he stood there, squinting through the bones of the skeleton house, trying to spot the path into the woods from a hundred yards away, trying not to look at the crows.

The kids lost interest in the new boy with the bright yellow bike. They rode back and took turns with their ramps and dirt piles and obstacles, even the boy with the sling.

The crows called at once, startling Josh out of the strange scene he'd found himself in. It was a ghost story, he thought. A group of kids telling about a house in the woods. A house at the end of a path that no one could go on. Crying walls. A murder of crows guarding the trail. That was a ghost story.

The crows called out again.

"Big Brother?" Josh whispered, still looking to the woods, hoping to see the path. He saw a flash of something—a bright shadow? Two eyes? But then it was gone, whatever he'd seen or hadn't seen.

The sky seemed darker when Josh turned to leave. He thought of those fairy tales, the scary ones, where a person wandered into a forest for an hour but it was really one hundred years. He waved goodbye to the kids, but they didn't notice. Their voices echoed behind him, laughing and shouting. He wondered about echoes, how they worked. For a moment he thought of them as real people, hiding in the forest and calling back whatever they heard. Echo people.

Josh was anxious to be home, but every turn put him on a street that, except for a flowerpot or a flagpole, looked just like his. It was like another bad fairy tale, or a nightmare, and his chest was beginning to get that tight feeling when he took another turn and found himself at the entrance to the development, right next to the waving bear. Josh let out a relieved breath. He knew how to get home from there.

He wondered if the kids were still out with their ramp, not far from a haunted house in the woods. He wondered if one of them was going to have to touch it. He shivered thinking of all the things around him, all the things he couldn't see.

WALLS

Josh set his bike in the corner of the garage, which still reeked of turpentine and spilled paint. "Mom?" he called.

He found her in the kitchen, holding an empty pot and a package of macaroni. Unopened boxes labeled KITCHEN were piled along the counters. Josh could tell she'd been worried but was trying not to show it. "How was your ride?"

"Good," he said. "I met some neighborhood kids."

"That's wonderful!" Her forehead lost its worried furrow. "Do they go to your school?"

"Yeah."

"That's wonderful!" she said again. "What did you all do? Did you ride somewhere?"

Josh didn't want to tell her about the house in the woods. The house where somebody died. "They had a ramp. They were doing jumps."

Worried again.

"Small ramps. They are younger than me."

"Oh. How young?"

He shrugged. "Maybe second grade. Or third."

"Well," she said. Her smile turned quivery. "That's a start. Your father will be so happy to hear you were riding your bike! Mac and cheese in ten minutes."

Later that night, Josh said good night to his mom. He went upstairs and got into bed, but was too scared to turn off the light. When he heard the phone ring, he knew it was his dad calling to check in. He also knew his parents would have a long, murmuring conversation about him.

Josh looked around at some of the posters his dad had given him over the years.

Push at your own edges

Stop playing it safe

Heroes are made not born

If you can't find the path, make one

When life gives you lemons, make lemonade

The posters, Josh suddenly saw, were arranged in this new room just as they'd been arranged in his old room. They'd moved all this way, to a new town and a new house for a new start, but he couldn't tell by looking at his room. He'd even picked the same color for the walls. What was the good of having inspirational posters if a person just tacked them back on a wall without looking? Without seeing? Without being inspired?

It made him think of the kids he'd met earlier, and the obstacle course. Why didn't he try it? What had he been afraid of? That he'd fall? That they'd laugh at him? Call him Kleenex?

He'd just been afraid for so long—and doing things the same way for so long—that he didn't know how to do anything differently. Would he ever? Or would he always surround himself with these same walls?

The more Josh stared at the posters and asked himself those questions, the more the walls seemed to close in. He heard his mom's footsteps coming up the stairs. She was still talking on the phone and he heard, "I'll just check if he's awake."

Josh jumped out of bed, raced across the room, turned off the light and dashed back. He was just pulling the covers up to his chin when he heard the faint knock on his door, then the click of the knob.

"Josh? Honey? You still awake?"

Josh froze, afraid she would know he was faking it. Then he wondered why he was faking it. Didn't he want to talk to his dad? He loved his dad.

He could pretend to wake up right then. He could. He could take the phone. He could tell his dad—tell his dad—tell him what? That Big Brother was back? That the invisible crack in the universe had somehow opened again? What would his dad say to that? What would his mom do? As he was pondering this, the door clicked shut. Josh heard more murmuring and then his mom's footsteps as they shuffled down the hallway.

He opened his eyes. The room was dark but one of his posters had a sparkly border that glowed in the dark, making it seem like a door to another world. The sparkles made him think about the girl from school, the one with the rainbow shirt and mismatched shoes. Would there be others?

"Big Brother," he whispered.

Back when Josh was younger, just a whisper like that was all it took. But things were different. He closed his eyes to block out the dark door with the sparkly border. It made him think of things he didn't want to think about. The kids with their obstacle course. The skeleton house. The path in the woods. School the next day.

He was drifting off to sleep when he remembered the rest. There was a house. A girl. Walls that cried. It was the right kind of ghost story. The spooky kind, the movie kind—the kind that everyone wanted to hear.

HIDDEN

The next morning Josh practiced in the mirror before going downstairs. "Mom, I'm going to ride my bike to school today." He said it to his reflection, making his face look serious but relaxed. Confidence!

He ran through the list of all the reasons why it was a good idea: excellent exercise; he was old enough; all the kids did it. He didn't know if the last one was true, but he had seen a bike rack with bikes near the bus zone.

Josh didn't want to lie to his parents, but they seemed to like the fake version of him better than the real one. Thinking about that made his eyebrows droop in an unconfident way. So he turned his back on the mirror and marched downstairs, straight to the kitchen. "Hey, Mom—"

His mom set down her coffee cup, glanced at his khaki

pants, and frowned. "Why aren't you wearing your new jeans? I washed them for you."

"I think you need to wash them again."

"Maybe you just don't like jeans." She poured milk over his cornflakes and held out the bowl. "You've always been a little particular. Remember when you couldn't wear pants at all? You had to wear shorts, even in the winter?"

"Yeah." Josh looked down at the cornflakes and took a deep breath. "So I'm going to ride my bike to school today." He tried to make his voice light, the way he'd practiced, and keep his eyebrows straight.

"No you're not," she said, as expected.

So Josh said, "Let's call Dad."

Ten minutes later, after he'd figured out how to adjust the seat and handlebars with the wrench he'd found in the box labeled TOOLS, Josh was riding down the road on his bright yellow SpongeBob SquarePants bicycle. "Big Brother," he whispered, "I hate you."

But a funny thing happened. The longer Josh was on his bike, the better he felt. His neck stopped twitching. His backpack felt lighter. Even the forest didn't seem so creepy. In no time at all, he was riding past The Last Stop, through town, and turning into the parking lot of Mountain View K–8.

He found the bike rack near the bus zone. A couple of

older kids were locking up their bikes and Josh braced himself for the teasing and laughter that would come when they looked at his bright-yellow one. But they didn't even glance his way.

Josh passed the gym doors and thought about the PE shorts in his backpack. He remembered the Friday tour with Ms. Yoshida, when she'd pointed out the lockers in the locker room. He'd missed PE on Monday, but knew he'd have to show up today. And it was the running unit. Just thinking about it made his chest tight.

The Hello Walk was crowded with kids talking and laughing and sharing their early-morning energy. He kept his eye out for Big Brother and thought he saw him leaning against a wall, talking to a girl, but when he got closer no one was there. He did see Liddy, the classmate who had volunteered to show him the ropes. She was in a corner with a group of kids, but she didn't see him, not even when he passed by. It was like his old school. Once he'd learned to be invisible, he didn't know how *not* to be.

Josh turned the corner and glanced at the place he'd eaten lunch the day before. Dead Melanie's bench was so hidden behind the giant rhododendron that, if Big Brother hadn't shown him, he would never have known it was there.

He wondered about the dead girl. About her name on the

bench. The spot made him sad, but not for her, really. When he tried to figure it out, his sadness, it was like a math problem he had no idea how to solve.

The first bell rang but Josh continued to stand and stare at the tiny spot of bench where he'd probably end up eating his lunch again that day. Already everything felt exactly the same.

Except Big Brother. That was different. That was a mystery. Like another impossible math problem in his head.

INVISIBLE GORILLA

During the first week of school, when Mr. K had introduced the Marvelous Mysteries project and was giving examples, he told the class about an experiment with a bunch of dogs and a guy named Pavlov. The dogs learned that when a bell rang, they would get food. For several weeks Pavlov would ring the bell and then give them food, so after a while they learned to expect food every time a bell rang. He knew this because of their saliva. When he stopped giving them food, they still drooled every time a bell rang.

This was one of those things that made Lucas love Mr. K's classroom. Because with a lot of teachers, even if they told him something interesting, he wouldn't think about it the rest of the day, and especially not three weeks later. But things that Mr. K taught them, like Pavlov's dogs, stayed with him. So on Wednesday when Mr. K walked into the room, clapping his hands in his rock-star way and everyone in class sat up straight, Lucas thought, That's it. We are just like Pavlov's dogs.

While Mr. K took attendance, the kids got busy with their morning work packets. But when he told them to take out their math workbooks, they shuffled their feet impatiently. "What's up?" he asked.

The whole class spoke at once: "You said you'd present your Marvelous Mystery project!" "We've been waiting!" "When are you going to do your Marvelous Mystery?"

Mr. K smiled and held up his hand. "Ready-set?"

"You-bet."

"Okay, put away those math books and get out your Marvelous Mystery notebooks. Has everyone finalized their topic?"

Most of the class said yes and a few said maybe. Lucas didn't answer. He studied his brainstorm sheet. His list was long and he really was interested in every single topic. How would he ever choose?

"Don't forget," a voice whispered. "The marvelous mystery of Maxie Moon."

Lucas jumped. He glanced sideways but didn't see her. He did see the boy in the red raincoat, and that startled him for a moment. He'd sort of forgotten about him.

Josh Duncan was looking down at his paper. He appeared to be drawing instead of writing. Lucas thought back to

Monday, when he'd first seen him running through the narrow space between the two buildings, along with the shadow boy.

He twisted to see the very back corner. Maxie wasn't there, but instead of feeling relieved, he worried. When would she pop up next? What would she ask him to do?

"Add me," she whispered. "Add me to your list." Was she really speaking or was it just in his head?

"Stop!" he said.

He hadn't known he was going to say it. He wasn't even sure he said it out loud until Mr. K said, "Lucas? Are you okay?" Mr. K looked at the students sitting closest to Lucas. They all shrugged.

"I'm fine, Mr. K." He picked up his pencil and pretended to write.

Mr. K clapped twice. "Okay! Let's do this. Are you all ready for Mr. K's Marvelous Mystery?"

Everyone shouted that they were. Lucas closed his notebook.

"Now, remember," Mr. K said, as soon as the class had settled down, "this is not how any of you need to do your projects. This is my project. And I chose it because I'm interested in human perception. I want each and every one of your projects to reflect your unique visions. Your interests. Your biggest questions and greatest mysteries."

Liddy raised her hand. "Should we take notes?"

"No," Mr. K said. "You'll need to focus your attention. I'm going to ask you to count basketballs."

"That's it?"

"That's it. Just count basketballs."

Mr. K got the computer and the screen ready. He gave his instructions using his slow and scientific voice. He told the class they were about to see two groups of basketball players: a team dressed in yellow and a team dressed in green. "Your job," he continued, "is to count how many times the yellow team dribbles the ball. Got it?"

The whole class nodded. Got it. When Mr. K turned off the lights, everyone leaned forward, ready to count. "Remember," he said, as he hit the button. "Focus on the team in yellow."

Lucas thought there would probably be running around and confusion, a blur of yellow and green, maybe like a quarter-under-the-cup trick, which he was freakishly amazing at. But it wasn't like that at all. It was just two teams, one yellow and one green, standing in a circle, calmly bouncing a basketball ball back and forth.

So Lucas locked his eyes on the yellow team. And he counted. One, two, three, four . . . but then . . . five, six . . . something strange happened.

A gorilla happened.

A gorilla—actually a person dressed in a gorilla suit—stepped into the middle of the circle. And the gorilla, he just stood there. He pounded on his chest a few times and then walked away.

Through it all the basketball players just kept bouncing.

Lucas lost track of the bounces. Because the gorilla! That was funny! That was a good one! He even started to laugh, but stopped when he noticed that no one else was laughing. He took a quick glance around the room. No one was doing anything but counting balls, just like Mr. K had told them to do.

What?

When the last ball bounced, Mr. K turned on the lights. "Well?"

Kids called out numbers.

What?

Mr. K held up his hand. "One at a time, please." He pointed to Carmen, sitting in the front row.

"Nineteen!"

He pointed to Rashid. "Seventeen."

Point, point, point. Owen, Sam, Angelo.

Sixteen, seventeen, twenty.

Mr. K said, "Did anyone see anything unusual?"

Silence.

"No one?"

Um, yeah . . . THERE—WAS—A—GORILLA!

But Lucas didn't shout it out like he wanted to. Because, well, was there a gorilla? Really? If no one else had seen it, was it actually there?

"Interesting," Maxie Moon whispered in his ear. "Very interesting."

Lucas put his head in his hands.

"We're going to watch it one more time," Mr. K said. He turned off the lights. "And this time, I want you to just watch the video. Don't worry about counting balls."

Lucas raised his head. Again, it was the same basketball players wearing yellow and green and again, they bounced the ball back and forth. Halfway through, just like before, the gorilla walked in.

The gorilla.

Only this time, everyone saw him. They shrieked. They called out "There's a gorilla!" When he beat his chest, just like before, everyone laughed.

They shouted, "That's not the same video, Mr. K!"

He turned on the lights and said calmly, "It's exactly the same."

"The gorilla was not there before, Mr. K!"

"It's the same video."

The class erupted. Except for Lucas. He was frozen.

Mr. K sat on the edge of his desk and leaned forward until all the talk and laughter stopped. "There's a name for what just happened," Mr. K said in his serious scientist voice. "It's called inattentional blindness. Can anyone guess what that means?"

Lucas picked up his pencil and wrote, *It means I am not losing my marbles.*

Liddy said, "It means we maybe can't see something that we should be able to see. Something right in front of us."

"But why? What was different between the two times we watched the video?"

"We were counting the balls?"

"Exactly! You were focusing on something else. Your brain was told you'd be seeing something else."

Lucas wrote, *I saw it. I saw the gorilla.*

Several kids called out, "You switched the video." And everyone went nuts again, shouting about the gorilla being there or not being there the first time.

Mr. K held up his hand. "It's easy to miss something you're not looking for. We do it all the time. Each one of us, every day."

He then talked about brains and vision. How every moment the brain has all these decisions to make about what to pay attention to and what to ignore. How a person can't possibly see everything that is right in front of them, so the brain has to choose what to see. And often, when people expect to see things a certain way, that's exactly how they'll see them.

"Things that don't fit with our expectations will often be ignored," he said. "Even a gorilla."

Even a gorilla.

The fluorescent light flickered and hummed overhead. Lucas suddenly noticed it and thought of something: It was there all the time, the fluorescent light, flickering and humming. So why did he only notice it sometimes?

He looked down at his pencil and paper.

Mr. K was going on about how drivers hit bicyclists in broad daylight because they don't see them.

And how lifeguards could be staring at a person in front of them and not recognize that person is drowning.

"What?"

"That's crazy!"

"How can that be?"

Mr. K clapped twice and the class fell silent. "How many times have you been looking for something, like in your sock drawer or your locker, and you can't find it. But then someone else points out that it's right there, in front of you. And it's been in front of you the whole time. Raise your hand if that's happened to you."

Nearly every kid put up a hand. Then the chatter started again.

"The world is full of invisibles," Mr. K said, raising his voice to be heard. "Simply because of our focus or attention or beliefs or perceptions. What we miss, every moment of the day—it would just blow your mind."

He said more things and gave more examples. And everyone kept talking. But the world had frozen for Lucas after one sentence. *The world is full of invisibles.*

He felt a fluttering in his ear, and then a whisper. "Capiche?"

PE

Three minutes. That's all it took for the world to turn upside down. That's how it felt, anyway, when Josh realized he was the only one who had seen the gorilla walk into Mr. K's Marvelous Mystery video. Upside down. Inside out.

They were all supposed to be counting basketball bounces. Josh had been doing it perfectly. Bounce, bounce, bounce.

Until the gorilla.

And then when Mr. K asked everyone how many bounces the yellow team had—or was it the green?—it didn't matter, because Josh had stopped counting when he'd seen the gorilla. But no one else had seen it. No one.

"The world is full of invisibles," Mr. K had said. "Simply because of our focus or attention or beliefs or perceptions. What we miss, every moment of the day—it would just blow your mind."

He said more things and gave more examples. And everyone kept talking. But Josh had flipped to a new page in his notebook. What was in his mind seemed to show up on the paper. And there were so many things!

He saw Big Brother and his mother and his father and inspirational posters tacked to his wall. He saw a carved wooden bear and a skeleton house. A SpongeBob bicycle, alien-ship library, and a murder of crows. He saw a girl with two different-colored shoes, the one he'd seen the day before. Her shirt was the same, with the sparkling rainbow. He saw a volcano, erupting all over everything.

So many thoughts were like bumper cars in his brain, crashing into one another with questions about atoms and ants and an old pirate ship captain with a wooden leg.

Well, well, well.

When Josh looked up, the classroom was nearly empty. Mr. K was still in front of the projector, talking to a boy with the name Hernandez printed on the back of his shirt. He grabbed his notebook, shoved it in his backpack, slipped out the door, and headed to the gym.

The world is full of invisibles, he told himself. *Like Big Brother. Like me.*

Josh went straight to the empty corner of the locker room, passing a bunch of kids changing into different T-shirts. He was still thinking about the gorilla when he took out his new combination lock, the one Ms. Yoshida had told him to bring. He fiddled with the combination.

15-17-5

He'd been practicing at home and it clicked open right away. He snapped it shut and twirled the dial again.

15-17-5

Was it someone's job to come up with different combinations? That would be an interesting job. Probably, he thought, a computer did it. But back before computers, did a person come up with them? Could combination locks be his Marvelous Mystery project? No. People would laugh.

And that was the problem with Marvelous Mysteries, Josh realized. Anything he thought was interesting would probably seem pretty dumb to most other people. Or worse—it would be weird. Especially to his classmates. Even back in kindergarten and the book about the bear in his den. While the other kids were looking at the picture of the den and the bear and the other forest animals, it was the shadows in the corners that had made Josh lean forward—lean forward and crawl into the circle.

Josh slumped. Then he sat straight up. Because something was weird. Something was wrong. It took him a moment to understand that the weird thing was not a sound. It was a lack of sound. The talking and laughing and lockers banging and toilets flushing—all of it had disappeared. Josh had been sitting there so long, just thinking about the kindergarten bear book, that everyone had already changed and headed out the doors to the big high school track across the playfield.

Like in an old-time movie, the fluorescent light flickered above his head, made a buzzing sound, and then a pop. The corner went dark. Josh stood up. He sat back down.

"Hello?" he called softly. No one answered.

He could hear his heart pounding in his ears—that's how quiet it was. So what if—what if he just didn't go? What would happen?

He played it out in his head. He imagined the very worst thing: that the PE teacher would alert Ms. Yoshida. She'd call his mom. Maybe she'd come pick him up and he would tell her—he would tell her what? The truth?

It didn't matter. Because after a while of sitting like that, Josh's heart went back to beating like normal. He heard drops of water from the faucets. He heard the creaks of cement walls and the clock's sharp snap every time another minute passed. He stood. Walked around the locker room. Each metal locker looked identical to the one next to it, and inside were the things supposedly worth locking up.

Josh thought, Would it really matter if I ended up with a green T-shirt instead of a blue? Would it make any difference?

He stopped in front of the giant poster, the one with the muscled runner guy breaking the victory string. Josh stared at his bulging arms that were raised in triumph.

The champion pushed forward with his chest. "You don't even get a participation ribbon for this day," he said. "You know that?"

"Well," Josh said finally, "you're just stuck there. No one even looks at you."

"You are. You're looking at me."

"Only because there's nothing else to look at."

"Yeah? Well, at least I'm stuck like this"—the poster champ puffed out his chest even more—"you're stuck like *that*, buddy." He didn't say it in a mean way. He actually winked at Josh when he said it, then threw back his head and crossed the finish line in the pretty awesome infinity loop that was his life.

Josh said, "That's not very inspirational. Maybe you are winning the race but you aren't really doing your job." Then he spun around quickly, so he could have the last word, and went straight back to his locker in the dark corner.

That's where he sat, twirling his combination lock, until voices, real voices of his classmates, filled the space again. Feet pounded, doors slammed, lockers clicked. The air smelled like sweat and grass and rain.

Josh slipped his arms into his backpack. He waited until he heard his classmates start to leave the locker room. He stood and walked out with them.

Nothing bad had happened. No one seemed to notice.

Except the poster guy. As Josh walked past, he extended his bulging arm in a friendly high-five position. But Josh pretended not to see.

EMPEROR'S NEW CLOTHES

It was the usual lunch table and the usual friends, but for Lucas right then, nothing felt usual. For one thing, Maxie Moon was doing some sort of weird dance in the middle of the cafeteria. No one else could see it, but still—it made Lucas so nervous his hands started to sweat.

And the other thing, of course, was the gorilla. Lucas was still thinking about Mr. K's class, and the gorilla experiment.

Right after class, he'd gone up to Mr. K to tell him what he'd seen. He'd waited until almost everyone else was gone. Then he cleared his throat and said, "I saw it."

Mr. K was fiddling with the computer but looked up right away. "The gorilla?"

Lucas nodded.

Mr. K leaned against the edge of his desk and crossed his arms over his chest. His "thinking look" as the kids called it. "Well, Lucas," he said finally. "Why didn't you say something?"

"I guess because when nobody else saw it, I wasn't sure."

"You weren't sure you were seeing the gorilla? Or you were afraid to be the first to say it? Or—"

Lucas shook his head. "I don't know," he said. "Maybe both. I don't know. It was weird."

Mr. K nodded and tapped his fingers. "Emperor's new clothes—do you know that story? When the tailors came to town and made the emperor clothes of a new fabric? Fabric so fine it was only visible to intelligent people? And the emperor paraded around naked, and no one said anything because they were all too afraid of being called stupid? Remember that story?"

"Yeah," Lucas said. He did.

"Speak up next time, okay? Like the kid in the story. You'd be surprised at how many more kids might follow."

Lucas could tell Mr. K wanted to talk more about the Emperor's New Clothes and speaking up and all that stuff that seemed to be favorite topics of grown-ups, so he said, "I need to get to PE."

"We can talk about this more in class, okay?" Lucas nodded but hoped Mr. K wouldn't call on him to talk about it.

And then in PE he ran around the track and was feeling good and Coach Wolfberg was shouting, "Good job,

Hernandez! Keep it up!" But then Maxie Moon appeared in the stands again, kicking her legs and dancing like a cheerleader.

"Go, Lucas, go!" she screamed. And Lucas faltered. He practically stopped. He bent over and sucked in air and watched the feet of his classmates thunder past him.

When he finally stood and walked the final stretch to the finish line Coach Wolfberg said, "You just need to pace yourself better at the beginning." And he nodded. Because what could he say?

Lunch was halfway over and his friends had finished eating and were busy gathering their trash and recycling. "You coming, Lucas?" they asked.

Lucas looked down at his sandwich. He hadn't even taken a bite. "Go ahead. I'll catch up with you."

He wasn't hungry, but he didn't feel like walking with them in their normal group. Everything felt too strange and twisted for that. He thought about Mr. K's class again, and the thing he'd said about the Emperor's New Clothes. Yes, Lucas knew the story. Practically everyone did. And it did make sense. Speaking up and all that. But there was something that had always bugged Lucas about that story.

What if the clothes really *were* invisible? What if they were spun from the most magical thread in the entire universe?

And what if everyone was too stupid to see? Including the stupid little kid who became the hero of the story?

From the middle of the cafeteria, Maxie Moon twirled around and waved at him again. Of course he couldn't have told Mr. K what he really thought. All he could do was nod and say yes, yes, next time he would certainly speak up because, of course, the Emperor's New Clothes!

FIRST MEETING

At lunchtime Josh got two slices of pizza again and walked out to Dead Melanie's bench. He picked off the pepperoni slices and stacked them on the side of the plate.

Tap, tap, tap.

He was thinking about several things at once: the invisible gorilla, his invisible locker-room experience, and the fact that pepperonis were so perfectly round they looked like freaky eyes.

Tap, tap, tap.

Did he hear them or see them? He wasn't sure. Did they really make a noise, or was it the motion that made them seem like they had? Two feet, right in front of him, in mismatched shoes.

Tap, tap, tap.

Josh looked up, just as the sun slid out from behind a

cloud. The air in front of him shimmered. Two shiny pots of gold on either side of a sparkly rainbow—that's what he saw after the shoes. And then she was there, hovering in front of him with her strange and watchful eyes. His heart did a fast flip and his neck started up again. SOS, the twitch warned.

He clamped his hand against his neck but still, SOS.

The world seemed to tilt, like a picture on its side. Josh wasn't hungry but he picked up his pizza because it was something to do. *I am choosing to ignore this,* he said to himself, just as Dr. Ted had instructed. But the dough and cheese was expanding in his mouth and the sun was blinding and there were those little shiny pots of gold. And his neck.

"I saw you in Mr. K's class today."

He stared at her feet. *Tap, tap, tap.*

"I know you can see me."

Josh stuffed more pizza in his mouth.

"And you saw the gorilla, too, didn't you?"

Josh closed his notebook. *You are not really here*, he said to himself, as he was supposed to.

"Do you want me to go?"

He continued to stare at her feet. Then slowly he said, "You don't need to go because you are not really here. You are not a part of the real world."

She laughed and tapped her shoes together. One green, one red. "You see me, don't you? Maybe *you're* not here. Maybe you're a dream. Maybe it's not even your own dream. Maybe you're part of *my* dream. Have you ever thought of that?"

Of course he had. *I am the dream of a giant fungus on a tree.* He cleared his throat. "I saw you before," he said.

"I know you did. And you saw the gorilla today."

"How do you know that?"

"I was there."

Josh looked up. The world was so bright. Her shirt was so sparkly. A crow landed on the garbage can on the far side of the bench and cocked its shiny head at them. Josh remembered to turn his face, so the crow wouldn't memorize it.

"Maybe we should start a club." The sparkly girl raised her hand in an official way. "First meeting of the Gorilla Club."

Even though he knew better, Josh said, "I was in a backgammon club at my old school. But I was the only one." His voice came out like a croak.

"That's sad. You won't be the only one in this club. Lucas Hernandez saw it, too. The gorilla. You should ask him. What did you do in your loser backgammon club?"

"Played backgammon. But because I was the only one, I played on the computer." He was going along with it, with her, and it was feeling too easy. The crack in the universe was expanding in an alarming way. "What does the Gorilla Club do?"

The girl tapped her toes and shrugged. "Whatever we

want. We have meetings. Maybe we go into the woods. You should ask Lucas."

"I don't know Lucas."

"He's in your class."

"I know but—" Josh shrugged.

"Why do you get pepperoni?"

"What?"

"You just pick them off. Why do you get pepperoni if you just pick them all off?"

Josh looked down at his plate with its neat stack of pepperoni slices.

"You need to learn to speak up for yourself."

Josh nodded. "I guess." She sounded way too much like Big Brother when he was being bossy. And it was strange to be talking to her. Talking out loud. It had been so many years without them, his friends. He knew it meant trouble, and soon. He tried to think of a poster that would help, but nothing came to mind. Except the sad cat clinging to the tree. Hang in There! That pretty much worked for anything.

"Nothing is wrong with me," he said. "Except all of you. You need to go away."

"I can't," she said sadly.

Something in the way she said it made him look at her. Closely. She seemed smaller somehow, like a little kid. And lonely. He recognized that, too.

"Why? Why can't you go away?" The crow flew down from the garbage can and did a little hop dance at her feet.

She narrowed her eyes. "I don't know," she said finally. When the crow cocked its head at her, she cocked her head back.

Josh looked away, through the spaces of the leaves on the giant bush, all the way over to the Hello Walk, where kids grouped together in tight clusters. He said, "I don't know where I'm going to eat my lunch in the winter."

"Is that why you're sitting on this bench? Because you don't know where else to sit?"

Josh nodded.

"Melanie Price," she said.

"We will never forget," Josh finished.

The girl sighed and shook her head. "Melanie died two weeks before her thirteenth birthday. She was crossing the street in the middle of the afternoon. She was in the crosswalk. The driver said he didn't even see her."

"Well," Josh said. It made him think of the pirate captain. Well, well, well. He wondered if that's how the old captain felt—blank and at a loss for words. Alone in a world he didn't understand.

"What does that remind you of?"

"What?" He had no idea what she was talking about.

"The driver? Not seeing her?"

"I don't really—"

"Mr. K's class? The gorilla!"

"Oh."

"Get it? He didn't see her. Even though it was daytime and she was in the crosswalk."

"Oh," Josh said again. The other world was starting to collide with the real world in a dizzying way, and that was something new. He needed her to go back to her other place. He could not let it all happen again.

"You need to leave now," Josh said. But the girl stayed where she was. Maybe, thought Josh, I am the fungus in her dream.

She said, "All her friends have all moved over to the high school."

"What?"

"Melanie Price. The girl whose bench this is. I guess her parents didn't think about that when they put up the bench— they didn't think about her friends growing up and leaving this school. Going to football games. Learning to drive."

"Well," Josh said, and then stopped himself from saying it two more times by taking in deep breaths.

The girl said something, but he didn't hear what it was. A wind tunnel, that's what it sounded like. Josh was tired. So tired.

"You need to go away now," he said. And he meant it. He

really did. He was looking at his own lumpish feet and thinking that maybe if he closed his eyes she would leave. Maybe she would slip back through that invisible crack that didn't make sense in this world. Maybe his life at this new school would have a chance of being normal.

He heard her say, "I know someone who wants to be your friend." And he opened his eyes.

But it was too late, then. She was gone. And the crow was gone, too.

What did that mean? She knew someone who wanted to be his friend? "Hey, Big Brother?" Josh whispered, but there was not even a breeze of a response.

As Josh walked to the garbage can on the far side of Dead Melanie's bench, he looked again to the Hello Walk, where the kids still clustered in groups. Some were just standing around talking, while others tossed balls and Frisbees. The girl was there, too, watching it all.

When she turned to look in Josh's direction, he lowered his eyes, dumped his lunch into the trash, and hurried away.

WAVE

Lucas couldn't make sense of the whispering in his ear. It was something about the new kid, the kid who wore the stupid red raincoat, even when it wasn't raining.

The kid was halfway hidden by a bush and a garbage can, but when Maxie pointed him out, Lucas recognized him. He ignored her and waved goodbye to his friends.

"Lucas!" his friends called. "Where you going? First bell hasn't even rung yet."

"I need to finish my math homework," Lucas lied. He really just needed to get away from her and her whispering and her pointing. He needed to be alone.

But she followed close behind him, talking fast. *Her mind moves a mile a minute.* That's what his abuela had always said about Maxie Moon. *Her mouth can't keep up with that brain of hers!* When she said it, she'd smiled. Everyone used to smile about Maxie.

Maxie Moon had stopped talking, but he knew she was still nearby. Lucas veered sharply into the chaos that was lunchtime in the Hello Walk. Kids crowded around him and pushed without even noticing. Lucas thought, I am the gorilla, and everyone is busy counting balls.

A feeling so big and so sad came in like a giant wave and knocked him off his feet. He looked down. He was still standing, but it felt like he was flat on his back on the cold cement floor.

Maxie Moon was in his ear again, buzzing again, talking about the house in the woods and the new boy again. Something about a Gorilla Club and what she wanted him to do. The house in the woods. The house in the woods. With the new boy. The house in the woods. Get him there.

He couldn't listen. He didn't want to listen. But then he heard her say, "Just do this one thing for me, and I'll go away. I'll leave you alone. I won't come back."

"What?" He spun around. There was no one there. "What?" he said, again and again. But she was gone.

SAD MONKEYS

A thing Josh never told his parents, or Dr. Ted, was that people, real people, made him nervous. So nervous that sometimes his eyes would freeze. He'd start staring at a random thing.

A shiny button.

Or an ear.

He would stand there, staring. At the ear. Or the button. And if he did manage to get his words out in the right order, his voice would sound weird. Also, if he stood there for very long, his face would get sweaty. It was probably why he chose to have conversations with things that weren't alive, like the wooden bear and the poster guy.

Josh decided it was time to make a change. Maybe it was his dad's poster quotes suddenly doing what they were supposed to do, or the surprise of Big Brother showing up again (and then disappearing for long stretches of time), or the mysterious sparkly girl with her cryptic message. Or maybe it was thinking about his mom at home with her rash and unpacked boxes.

But whatever had prompted his desire to make a change—a big one—Josh was ready. Ready to enter the real world, with real people.

The thing was, he didn't know it would be so hard.

Hard to raise his hand in class.

Hard to make eye contact.

Hard to find a seat in the cafeteria.

After a few days, he just stopped trying. He didn't see the sparkly girl again, even though he looked for her everywhere.

Because of Dead Melanie's bench, lunch at his new school wasn't a problem. At least, not during that first week. But by the middle of the second week, when there was a new damp chill in the air, Josh wondered how much longer he'd be able to eat his lunch outside, behind a bush. He scouted out other hiding places, like he had at his old school. The bathroom was obvious. The locker room might be okay. And when he saw the DO NOT ENTER sign on the door that led to the old library stairwell, he wondered: Could that be it, the perfect lunchtime getaway?

He tried to conjure Big Brother, to talk it over, but Big Brother wasn't predictable the way he used to be. Instead he just showed up when he wanted to, sounding way too much like Josh's dad, and then—poof—was gone.

But even bossy, unpredictable, poster-quoting Big Brother was better than no Big Brother at all. So when he showed up at lunch that day, Josh sat up straight and grinned. He was so happy he couldn't even pretend to be mad. "Hey," he said. "Where have you been?"

Big Brother settled down on the bench. He was carrying an umbrella. "Aren't you getting wet?"

"Nah." Josh held up his hands. "Remember? We call it liquid sunshine!"

Big Brother laughed. "You missed picture retakes."

"What?"

"Picture retakes."

"That was today?" Josh thought back to the first day, when he'd seen the notice on the Mountain View K–8 reader board with his mom. It seemed like such a long time ago.

"Mom will be mad. She loves pictures of you." There was something sad about the way he said it.

"I'm sorry—" Josh started, but Big Brother held up his hand.

"Never mind all that. How is everything going?"

Josh shrugged. "Okay. Riding my bike is pretty good. You were right about that. But seriously, where are you all the time? Why is everything so different than it used to be?"

"We're both older. And I was gone for so long—"

Josh's throat tightened. In his mind he saw the awful dirt hole where he'd buried him, the little rock painted with his name. "I'm sorry. I told you—"

Big Brother didn't let him finish. "I'm not mad. I'm just glad to be back with you."

Josh cleared his throat. "Me too. I'm just glad you're back, too."

"And you haven't told Mom about me?"

"No," Josh said. "I'm going to wait until Dad gets back and tell them together."

"One fell swoop!"

"Exactly."

"Eat your pizza."

Suddenly hungry, Josh plucked off a pepperoni and bit into the thick, cheesy slice. Everything felt fine to him then. Even the sun came out from behind a gray cloud, lighting up the mist in sort of a magical way. He remembered to wipe the pizza grease from his mouth. "Hey, I thought I saw you talking to someone the other day. Over by that wall."

"Yeah?"

"Yeah. Who was she?"

"Let's see your notebook," Big Brother said, slyly changing the subject. "Did you pick a Marvelous Mystery topic yet?"

"Not yet." Josh pulled out his notebook and flipped it

open, to a page with a drawing of a baby monkey. "Liddy Franklin gave her presentation today."

"Wasn't she your buddy? Your show-the-ropes buddy?"

When Josh laughed, a glob of cheese flew out of his mouth and landed on his shoe. "Right. My buddy."

Big Brother said, "So what's with the monkey?"

Josh shook his head. Liddy had tried to find something similar to Mr. K's marvelous gorilla experiment, but her presentation had made the whole class want to cry. "Trust me. You don't want to know."

"Hey," Big Brother said. "If you can't tell your big brother about it, who can you tell?" And that's how Josh Duncan found himself sitting on a dead girl's bench, describing a monkey experiment that happened back in the 1950s.

"The experiment—it was all about loneliness," he started. "And it was old. Liddy had found an old film online. In black and white." The look of it had made most of the other kids laugh. To Josh, though, something about the old film seemed more real than color. Or maybe it was just that the scientists, who wore stiff white lab coats, looked totally sinister when the light glinted off their black-rimmed glasses.

"What happened was, they took the baby monkeys away from their living mothers and gave them wire mothers. The wire mothers all had bottles of milk attached to them, so the babies wouldn't starve. One group of wire mothers was covered with soft cloth, and the other was just plain wire, like a bunch of coat hangers in the shape of a monkey."

Josh flipped to a new page in his notebook, with more pictures he'd drawn. "The baby monkeys who got the soft cloth mothers turned out okay. They could even rejoin society and make friends with other monkeys. But the ones who had the cold, plain wire mothers couldn't be socialized. Ever." He closed his notebook. "That's all."

"That's awful," Big Brother said.

"It was bad," Josh agreed. "One kid cried."

"I'm sorry about the monkeys."

Josh swallowed. His throat was tight. "Me too."

"You are not a monkey," Big Brother said finally. "You have an invisible big brother who followed you across the country because he loves you."

Josh smiled. Big Brother knew what he was thinking.

"You will not be a sad monkey," he continued. "You will be a happy monkey. Okay?"

Josh nodded.

"And you know how? How you're going to be a happy monkey?"

"How?"

"You're going to make a friend."

"I've been trying."

"What's your next class?"

"PE."

"What are you doing in PE?"

"It's the running unit. A mile around the track."

"That's great."

Josh shoved the last of the pizza in his mouth. "You know I don't run. I got Mom to write me a note."

"You ran that first day, remember? You were fast."

Josh shrugged. "That was for survival. To get away from this place. And there was no one around to make fun of me."

"I think you should give it a try," Big Brother said. "And also, you should join a club."

Josh laughed out another glob of cheese. He reached down to pick both globs from his shoe. "Gorilla Club," he said, remembering the sparkly girl.

When he sat back up, Big Brother was gone. "Hey!" Josh said. "Where are you?"

He scooted down the bench and peered through the green leaves of the rhododendron plant. He didn't see Big Brother but he saw kids all around. And then he saw her again—the girl. She was on the other side of the Hello Walk, still wearing her sparkly rainbow T-shirt and mismatched shoes.

Something about her made Josh nervous. He'd never felt that before, with any of them. When he leaned forward for a better view, she turned and stared right at him. A strange smile formed at the corners of her mouth. She held up her finger and pointed.

It started to rain and there was a mad dash to the Hello Walk for cover. But Josh stayed on the bench, frozen by her stare and pointing finger. Then her finger curved. It beckoned.

Follow me.

THE NOTE

It was the one thing Lucas needed to do and then she'd go away. Forever. That's what she promised.

"Easy-peasy, stick to the plan," Maxie Moon whispered in his ear. "Capiche?" But Lucas did not capiche, not exactly. He knew what he needed to do, but it was hard to break away from his friends. He didn't want a lot of questions. He didn't want to explain anything about the note. He didn't want to even think about it.

When the rain started, it was one of those downpours that turns on full blast and without warning. His friends all pulled up their hoods and dashed for the cover of the Hello Walk. That's when Lucas saw his chance. He pulled up his own hood, but turned the opposite way, toward the bench where Maxie Moon told him he'd find the kid.

Lucas had the note in his pocket, the one she'd carefully

dictated—word for word—while she looked over his shoulder and breathed in his ear. "And draw the map," she said. He drew the map.

He would hand it to Josh Duncan and then he'd be done. Because that's what she promised. She promised to go away if Lucas did what she asked.

There was a question, of course, of what she really wanted. The contents of the note made Lucas worried for the red rain-coat boy. But Maxie Moon made a vow—a pinkie promise—that she wouldn't hurt the kid or do anything destructive ("What can I do, anyway?") and that she'd go away and leave him, Lucas, alone if he helped her.

"All I need to do is write this note and give it to Josh Duncan?" he asked, for the third time.

"That's all you need to do."

Easy-peasy, right? Except the closer Lucas got to the bench, the slower he moved. Was he really going to hand the note to the kid? What was he supposed to say when he did it? And what about the poor kid—did he really want him to do what Maxie had planned? And what *was* Maxie Moon's plan, anyway? Her real plan?

These thoughts and questions were like thick muck Lucas had to wade through. They made him walk so slowly he almost felt he wasn't moving at all. Like a cartoon character. Finally, though, through the thick muck of his thoughts, he reached the rhododendron plant. He still didn't know exactly how he would explain the note, but he was ready to hand it over. Did he have a choice?

Taking a deep breath, Lucas stepped around the overgrown bush. He opened his mouth to speak, but the boy in the red raincoat was gone.

Lucas stood in the rain, clutched the note in his hand, and stared at the empty bench with the sad engraving. MELANIE PRICE—WE WILL NEVER FORGET.

DO NOT ENTER

Hello, hello. Hello, hello.

Hands, feet, eyes. Elbows, mouths, hair. His first time actually going through the Hello Walk was every bit as bad as Josh had imagined. And the shifting tectonic plates—Josh could practically *feel* them rumbling deep underneath the cement slab.

Still, he kept going, pushing past kids who didn't notice him, keeping his eyes on the sparkly shirt. He had to know what she meant by the things she said. He had to follow that beckoning finger.

Wherever a gap appeared, Josh squeezed through. Finally, he made it to the other side. But when he looked around, the girl was gone.

Why would she motion for him to follow, and then disappear? Where would she go?

Mr. K's gorilla experiment suddenly came to mind. *It takes careful attention to see what is really in front of you.* Josh closed his eyes. Then he opened them. And that's when he saw the door—the door to the stairwell that led up to the old library. He'd been standing right in front of it the whole time without actually seeing it.

DO NOT ENTER.

He took another quick look around. She had wanted him to follow her. Is this where she went? The old library?

Josh's parents had lectured him about the dangers and pitfalls he was about to encounter as he approached his teenage years. He knew that "The only way to get through was to get through" (Dad), and that you should "Never put off until tomorrow what you can do today" (Dad), and that "Heroes are made not born" (poster from Dad), and that only he could "Be the hero" of his own story (poster on locker room wall that he hoped his dad would never see), and "Don't do anything that will put you in the hospital" (Mom). But Josh didn't have a quote to help him through a situation like this one.

Or did he? Weren't all those quotes (except for his mom's) telling him to put himself out there? Take a risk? Open a door? He stared at his limp hand, which didn't seem at all like an inspirational-poster hand.

Move, he said to the hand. Just do it.

Because there was one more thing, a bigger thing that Josh

was beginning to feel. It wasn't about being a hero. As much as he wanted it to be, this wasn't his hero story at all. It was about being alone. Sometimes alone is fine and sometimes it is not. Right then, Josh was a tiny boat out on the vast ocean without an anchor. It reminded him of another thing his dad quoted from Benjamin Franklin: "A small leak will sink a great ship." It was exactly that—the small leak of loneliness—that was sinking his ship. Josh knew it. He felt it. And at that very moment, he was the only one who could plug it.

Even though she wasn't a part of the real world, Josh had liked it when the girl talked to him. But it was confusing, too. The Gorilla Club and Lucas Hernandez seemed like scattered pieces from different puzzles. And Big Brother. He was from another puzzle, too. And yet somehow, they seemed like they should fit together. Josh had the strange feeling that she might know how.

He counted to seven because seven was a lucky number. He needed the luck of an unlocked door. And then he counted to fourteen, because that seemed like it would be double lucky.

He heard a bell ring, and it must have meant something to all the kids running to class. But right then it meant nothing to him. Because right then, Josh was testing his luck. He pushed on the handle of the door and it opened with a click.

Life is a glorious adventure.

Or it is nothing.

GREAT-AUNT EVELYN

With each step up the concrete stairway Josh heard another step—an echo step behind his own. It sounded so real that he finally stopped and looked back, but there was nothing. Just the swirling dust from his own shuffling feet.

Because of his alien-ship first impressions, Josh had expected to discover something spectacular at the top of the plain gray stairwell. Instead, he was disappointed by the small foyer with plain gray walls, dusty tile floors, and double-glass doors that led to the old library. Standing there, he couldn't even tell he was aboveground.

It was quiet, though, in a spectacular kind of way. If there was such a thing as a negative quiet, that's what it was. For a moment Josh felt he wasn't even a part of the world anymore. The real world, at least.

He stepped close and pressed his nose against the glass

door. Even though the room was dark, the longer he stood like that, the more he could make out shapes. He saw tables and chairs. Bookshelves with a scattering of left-behind books. He didn't see the sparkly girl.

Still, he stayed and stared at the shapes of left-behind things. It was like studying those pictures of Pompeii after Mount Vesuvius blew up and all those people and dogs and loaves of bread were petrified. And then he caught a glimpse of his own reflection and it startled him. He looked like someone else, someone he didn't know. Quickly, he pushed open the door.

The dirty skylights, along with a few high windows, let in enough light to help navigate around random tables and stacks of chairs. Josh found a light switch and almost turned it on but stopped himself. Someone might see.

He stumbled over to the nearest wall and inched along, running his hands over the scattered spines of books left behind. "Hello?" he whispered. "Hello?" But except for old wooden furniture and dusty books, the library was empty.

He stopped in the far corner, which was the darkest part of the library. He felt off balance and clutched the dusty shelf. He pictured the Hello Walk below. What if an earthquake hit? Why hadn't he thought of that?

The idea was suddenly so real in his head that his legs wobbled and he had to sit down. After a moment of sitting in the dark, the silence of the library did some sort of magic on him. He felt calm.

He knew he needed to go back down, but he didn't want to hear his feet echo through the empty hallway, and he didn't want to walk into class fifteen minutes late with everybody looking—or not looking. Either way. So he leaned his back against the bookshelf. As his eyes adjusted to the dark, Josh reached behind and pulled down a stack of books, blew off thick layers of dust, and made a neat pile. One by one, he went through them, setting aside the books he wanted to check out.

There was one about Harry Houdini, the most famous escape artist of all time. Josh and his dad had big debates over Harry Houdini, because Josh thought he was a hero and his dad said he was just a guy who knew a few tricks. Josh slipped *Harry Houdini* inside his backpack.

He also kept a book about the 1980 eruption of Mount St. Helens, of course. And one about land snails and slugs of the Pacific Northwest. And one about Muhammad Ali, who was most definitely a champion. He and his dad had no argument over that.

It was when he picked up the next book that he heard the voice. At first he didn't notice. But when he held it close to read the title, *Beloved Poems* by Robert Frost, he heard the voice again.

"That's the one."

Josh looked up. An old lady stood in front of him. His heart thumped and he clutched at his chest. He wondered if he was having a heart attack. Could an eleven-year-old have a heart attack?

The old lady was one of those sporty types. Her Adidas tracksuit was so bright that, even in the dim light, it glowed red.

"I'm sorry I'm up here," Josh said, still clutching his chest. "I know I'm not supposed to be."

The old lady didn't answer.

"Um, are you the librarian?"

She still didn't answer.

Josh dropped the book of poetry and started to stand, but the old lady held up her hand. It was knotted like an ancient oak branch. "The book," she whispered.

"What?"

"The one you were holding." Her tree-limb finger pointed to the ground. "The book of poems."

Josh picked it up.

"Open it," she said.

Josh opened the cover to a shaky inscription: *To my wonderful nephew, Jackie. Happy Birthday. With Buckets of Love from Great-Aunt Evelyn.*

"'Stopping by Woods,'" she rasped. "Tell me the page."

Josh's hands were shaking, but he managed to open the book to the table of contents. "Page twenty-four," he said, because he didn't know what else to do.

"Well?"

"Um—"

"Open it."

Josh flipped to the poem and right there, like a secret bookmark, was a ten-dollar bill. What?! He looked up quickly. The old lady winked.

Smooth and crisp with Alexander Hamilton's revolutionary face, the bill looked like it had never been touched. The old lady leaned close. While one of her eyes wandered to the poem on the open page, the other stared straight ahead. Josh waited for her to speak.

And waited.

He remembered he might be having a heart attack. "Are you the librarian?" he finally stuttered. "Am I in trouble for being here?"

"You're in no trouble with me," she said. "I've been waiting for someone like you for a very long time. Read me the poem."

So he did. Because he didn't know what else to do, he cleared his throat and started reading to the old lady.

Whose woods these are I think I know.
His house is in the village though;
He will not see me stopping here
To watch his woods fill up with snow.

Josh paused. Did she want him to read the whole thing? When he looked up for clarification, her pale watery eyes were way too close to his own. He stepped back until the hard edge of a bookshelf pressed against his shoulder blades.

"It's for my Jackie," the old lady whispered, her wandering eye landing on the ten-dollar bill clutched in Josh's hand. "He never knew it was in there. He left the book here, in the library. He didn't know about the money inside."

"Oh no," Josh moaned when he realized. She was not the old librarian. She was not a teacher. It was the invisible crack again.

Josh felt his chest squeeze even tighter. He dropped to his knees and fumbled with the zipper on his backpack. He needed his inhaler. He told himself, "I will close my eyes and when I open them, she will be gone. Because she was never here in the first place. She is not a real person in the real world. She does not belong here."

He took a breath. Opened his eyes.

Great-Aunt Evelyn's feet, marching in place.

He looked up.

Great-Aunt Evelyn in her red tracksuit.

She was doing arm exercises, first little circles and then big ones. And she was laughing. Her mouth was wide-open, but no sound was coming out.

He dropped the book, and the money, too, grabbed the strap of his backpack and bolted for the door.

But she was right there, blocking.

Each way Josh tried to go, the old lady was blocking. And she was no longer laughing. "I'm sorry," she whispered firmly. "But I won't leave you alone until you take the money. I will follow you forever. Just put it in your pocket, so you'll have it if you ever run into my Jackie. He goes by Jack now, and he's all grown up. But I call him Jackie. I always will."

Josh shook his head, side to side, and stood there with Great-Aunt Evelyn, toe to toe. He sucked in a tight, wheezy breath. "You are not really here," he said firmly, straight into the one eye that managed to meet his own. "And if you come around again, I will have to bury you. In my backyard. I've done it before."

She nodded wildly, like a half-broken bobblehead doll. "You can bury us all. But until you do what you need to do, we'll come back. Each and every one of us." She started to hum.

"What do I need to do?" Josh was practically crying. "What is it?"

"My Jackie would have liked that ten dollars. He never even knew about it. He thought I just gave him a book of poems. He was my favorite nephew. I'd like him to know that."

Josh went to slide the bill back into the book, but her raspy voice stopped him. "You can fold it. Put it in your pocket and keep it there. You never know when you might run into him. When you do, give him the money. From me. Keep the book for yourself. Because you are a good boy."

With trembling hands Josh folded the bill and shoved it deep into the front pocket of his khaki pants. The old lady's one good eye shone gratefully into his. "Thank you," she said, but there was no longer any sound. Just her lips moving, her mouth opening and closing, and then she was gone.

Josh wanted to leave the book behind but was afraid she would come back if he did, so he slipped it in his backpack, along with the four other left-behind books that were already there. And even though Great-Aunt Evelyn was not real, not real, he ran in a big circle around the place she had been.

DISAPPEARED

"Did you do it?"

"I tried. I went over there, when it started to rain. But he wasn't on the bench. He had already gone. It was like he disappeared."

"Do you still have the note?"

"Yes."

"Tomorrow. You need to do it tomorrow. Capiche?"

"I will. I will. And then you will go away, right? Like you said? And you won't come back again?"

Maxie Moon didn't answer. She was already gone.

MILES TO GO

Josh should have told his mom, right away. The minute Big Brother first appeared again. He should have told her before the sparkly girl and the scary old lady in the tracksuit. He should have told her everything.

But . . .

He would tell her now. He would ride like the wind on his SpongeBob bicycle and he would march right in and show her the book of poetry. And he would tell her about the ten-dollar bill and Great-Aunt Evelyn and everything else he'd been hiding since the move.

Josh dropped his bike on the front lawn, sprinted for the door and burst inside. "Mom!" he shouted. "Mom!"

She must have heard the panic in his voice because she ran, too. They collided in the hallway and Josh fell back against the wall.

His mom grabbed him by his shoulders and held on tight. "Josh! Are you okay? What's the matter?"

He opened and closed his mouth, like a fish that had jumped out of its tank. "I'm fine," he gasped. "But—"

"Come on." She helped him out of his wet raincoat and led him down the hallway into the living room. "You need to catch your breath first," she said, guiding him to the couch. "Just relax, honey. And then tell me everything." While she waited, she patted his back, like when he was little and having an asthma attack.

"Where's your inhaler?"

Josh motioned to his backpack. Then he did the regular stuff to calm himself. He ran through the multiples of 3 up to 99, named the fifty states in alphabetical order backward, and sang "Mary Had a Little Lamb," all in his head.

And it was starting to work. Just being on the couch, safe with his mom, the other stuff didn't seem so bad. "Okay," he said. "I have something to tell you."

Josh's mom looked straight into his eyes and smiled, but it was the quivery brave smile. "You know you can tell me anything, honey. We can deal with anything that's going on with you." She scratched her wrist.

To avoid the terrible smile and the rash peeking out from the end of her sleeve, Josh glanced around the room. It was mostly still filled with labeled boxes, but one was open. And there were photographs hanging on the wall. "Hey," he said. "What did you do?"

His mom's mouth managed to keep its quivery brave shape when she said, "What do you mean?"

"The wall."

"I unpacked our photos today. I put them up."

"Did you finish the kitchen?"

She shook her head.

His mom had a thing about photos on the wall. Josh thought it was her way of proving that they were a normal, happy family.

There was Josh as a baby, taking his first steps.

Josh on his first day of kindergarten.

Josh and Dad fishing.

Josh in third grade, with his brand-new SpongeBob bicycle that he got for his birthday. There were all his school pictures, lined up in order.

His neck twitched. "Why did you hang them like that?"

"What do you mean?"

"Every picture is in the exact place it was before. It's like we never moved." As he said it, he thought again about the inspirational posters in his own room, how he'd done the same thing. "What's the point of moving if nothing changes?" Josh's voice was an octave higher than he thought it could go.

"Josh, honey, what do you need to tell me?" He looked

down and saw her hand, patting his knee. He wondered if the nervous rash was contagious. Even if it wasn't, he didn't want it to touch him.

He opened his mouth to speak, but took another look at the wall of happy family photographs. The Thanksgiving when Gran and Pops were still alive. The time when it snowed so much that Dad stayed home from work to make a snow fort.

And the one sad one, the baby one.

A shiver ran up and down his back. In the photo his mom is looking down at the baby, her hair so long it nearly reaches his tiny face. One baby fist is raised in a cute and funny way. It had always been on the wall with all the other photos, but Josh had stopped seeing it years before.

Still, he knew the basic story. The baby was born four years before Josh. There was something wrong with his heart. He died before his first birthday.

His parents didn't like to talk about him, so Josh had learned to stop asking. And then Big Brother had showed up on that first day of kindergarten, followed by all the others, and it wasn't that Josh didn't try to work out the pieces to the puzzle—it was more that he'd never seen there *was* a puzzle.

Now he leaned in for a closer look. When he did, he almost laughed out loud. Because there was Big Brother, up against the wall, posing! Like he was a wall photo, too. He winked and whispered, "Don't do it, Little Bro." Then he changed positions, so he was next to the photo of Dad and Josh with fishing poles. He held up his hands, pretending to measure his own enormous fish. That did it—Josh *did* laugh out loud.

His mom snapped her head. "What's so funny?"

"Nothing, Mom."

"Josh? What are you laughing at? What were you going to tell me?"

"Don't do it," Big Brother whispered again. "Don't tell her. If you do, I'll have to go away, and I'm not ready for that. You're not ready for that."

"Mom," Josh said, closing his eyes so he wouldn't have to see Big Brother's face. "I haven't been completely honest with you."

"Little Bro," he pleaded. "We're not done yet. We have miles to go before we sleep."

"What?"

"I didn't say anything, Josh. You did."

"Right. Mom. I know. As I was saying—" Josh opened his eyes and looked back at the wall of photographs. Big Brother had changed his position and was not trying to be a photo anymore. Instead he was just looking at Josh in a pleading way.

He was his best friend. He was his brother.

Big Brother clasped his hands together and mouthed the word *Please?*

"It's nothing terrible, Mom," Josh said. "Just, well. I haven't been eating in the cafeteria."

"What?"

"That buddy thing never worked out and I couldn't find a place to sit. So I've been sitting outside, on a bench—"

"Wait, you've been eating outside, on a bench? In the rain?" Josh had never seen his mom look so relieved in her life. She was so relieved she had to pretend to look concerned. "Is anything else going on? Are you hiding out again?"

"No, Mom. I mean, PE that once."

"But you're home early. Why? What happened?"

"Mom, nothing. I just—I'm sorry. I'm sorry I don't have friends to bring home. And birthday parties to go to. I'm sorry."

"Oh, Josh." She pulled him close. "You don't have to be sorry about anything. We can deal with this. Everything is going to be fine."

Josh knew his dad would have something much more inspirational to say, and he was glad he didn't have to hear it. "Thanks, Mom," he said. He so wanted to tell her the truth, about everything. But he couldn't. Not then.

He pulled back and made a move to leave. Then he noticed that his mom was staring past his shoulder at the wall of family photos. It was like she'd forgotten about him, and her face had an expression he couldn't name. Worried, puzzled, startled, sad—he couldn't tell what.

"What is it, Mom? What's the matter?"

"Nothing. Nothing at all." But she rubbed her arms and shivered, like some sort of shadow had filled the room.

"Mom? Are you okay?"

She nodded. "I think I've just been staring at old photos too long today." She glanced at the baby photo and opened her mouth to say something more.

Josh held his breath, just hoping. Hoping they could talk about the baby and the box of baby things and all the invisible things they lived with, every day. But she scratched her wrist and said, "Do you have homework?"

"Yes," Josh said. "I'm going to my room."

"I'll call you for dinner."

That was it.

Josh went to his room but his room wasn't big enough anymore. Like when Alice goes to Wonderland and eats that thing or drinks it—he couldn't remember which—and then she grows until she's completely busting out of the room. That's how he felt.

"Big Brother," he whispered, "I did what you asked. Where are you?" But he didn't come.

He took the stolen library books from his backpack and stacked them next to his bed, with the poetry book by Robert

Frost on top. Josh stayed that way, just getting used to it. It was a technique Dr. Ted had taught him, for being scared of things like dogs and spiders and crowds.

Finally, when he was used to the book being there, he reached over and opened the cover. He stared at the inscription, remembering those gnarled old hands and the crazy eye. *To my wonderful nephew, Jackie. Happy Birthday. With Buckets of Love from Great-Aunt Evelyn.*

Pulling the ten-dollar bill from his pocket, he flattened it smooth and slipped it back into the book. Then he read the first stanza of the poem again. He read the second stanza, too, whispering the words to himself and listening closely for some kind of clue, some kind of answer to his big questions about Big Brother and the sparkly girl and the old lady and his mom's rash and his dad's posters and the invisible gorilla and all of it.

My little horse must think it queer
To stop without a farmhouse near
Between the woods and frozen lake
The darkest evening of the year.

The air around Josh felt suddenly cold, but in a good way, like he was inside the poem and could see his breath make a puff of cloud on that winter's night. Like from across the miles and years, Mr. Robert Frost was reaching out and speaking directly to him, Joshua Duncan, fifth grade.

"Mr. Robert Frost," Josh said out loud. His voice sounded like a stranger's voice as he continued to read the poem in a whisper.

> *The woods are lovely, dark and deep,*
> *But I have promises to keep,*
> *And miles to go before I sleep,*
> *And miles to go before I sleep.*

Miles to go? Before we sleep? Those were the exact words Big Brother had used when he was being all funny next to the photographs.

It was all so different than it used to be. It was like Big Brother wasn't just hanging around to build Lego worlds and play moon landing anymore.

Josh jumped up and paced the room. Then he got out his huge box of Lego and dumped it on the ground for sorting. By the time his mom called him down for dinner he had all the blues in one pile and a good start of the reds, and the world felt normal—almost—again.

His mom made meat loaf for dinner. She was excited because she found a recipe website for one-pan meals. Josh wanted to ask why they didn't just unpack all the kitchen boxes so they'd have more than one pan, but he had a feeling it would lead to more itching of the rash.

His dad called later, when they were washing the one pan and two plates. He was calling from Japan, where it was only lunchtime, but already the next day. "You're like a time traveler," Josh said, and his dad laughed.

"What have you been doing? How's school?"

Josh told him everything was fine and that he was riding his bike everywhere.

"That's great, Josh. What else has been going on?"

"I got some good books today. One about Muhammad Ali."

"Float like a butterfly. Sting like a bee!"

Josh laughed. "And I got another one of your favorites."

"Yeah? Who?"

"Harry Houdini."

"Harry Houdini! You know how I feel about Harry Houdini."

"You mean the greatest magician of all time?"

"I mean a guy who had a few tricks."

Josh knew the conversation, practically word for word. It was as warm and comfortable to him as an old favorite sweater. They went back and forth like that, about Harry Houdini, until Josh forgot the big secret he was keeping. But then his dad said, "First thing when I get home? We're going to buy you a new bike. What do you think about that?"

And Josh remembered that it was Big Brother who got him out riding. Big Brother—who wasn't supposed to be there.

"That's great, Dad," Josh said. "Really great." And it actually was great. He was not lying about that.

DEADLINE

It was Friday, and Lucas was supposed to give his Marvelous Mystery presentation the following Monday. Back during the first week of school, when the sign-up sheet was going around, October had seemed like years away. Lucas knew there'd be plenty of time to pick a topic and put together a presentation. But that was before everything got turned upside down with Maxie Moon.

Now Lucas couldn't think about anything *but* Maxie Moon. And the note. And the new kid. "Why?" he'd asked her. "Why the new kid?"

"Because he saw the gorilla, too," she said. "Capiche?" And that was it.

Even when she wasn't there, buzzing in his ear, he was jumpy and nervous, just waiting for her to show up and freak him out. Anytime he saw something sparkly or a flash of light around the corner, he broke out in a sweat. Even in Mr. K's class he had a hard time paying attention to anything anyone was saying.

There were a few giggles and when Lucas looked up, he saw that everyone was staring at him. "I'm sorry—" he started.

Mr. K stood at the front of the room. He waved his clipboard and sign-up sheet. "I was just asking about Monday, Lucas. I haven't seen your rough draft or even your topic yet. Are you set for your presentation?"

Lucas nodded.

Why did he do that? Why didn't he just ask for more time? Lucas stared down at his brainstorm sheet, but the words all blurred together.

Mr. K said, "Well, I'm looking forward to it. And to being surprised by your topic."

"Oh, he'll be surprised," Maxie buzzed in his ear. "We all will."

He went on to ask for questions. "Anything?" Mr. K said. "Anyone have any questions about their presentations?"

"I don't know which topic I should choose. My brainstorm list is too long." Several of his classmates shared that problem.

"Pick the topic that jumps out at you," Mr. K said. And then, "Boo!" as he jumped forward at them. The class laughed. All except Lucas.

"Or pick the topic that seems the hardest. Challenge

yourselves. Or one that scares you. Pick one you have no idea how it will come out."

The problem, Lucas realized when the bell rang and he was putting his notebook away, the problem was that the biggest mystery in his life wasn't one he could talk about. It wasn't one he could research and study and understand. It was also a topic that he tried his best to forget.

For years, right around this very time, something would happen—something that made him remember her. He'd see an interesting rock and remember how they used to spend hours in the woods, looking for rocks to add to their shared collection. Or he'd hear a bit of Italian, and remember how Maxie's nonna would try to feed them salami sandwiches every time they came home from school together.

And then, when the stories started about the house in the woods, it was impossible not to think about her.

The stories were frightening, and couldn't be real. But with each new family that moved in, the stories continued. Stories of books dropping from shelves. Doors slamming in the middle of the night. And crying, always crying, coming from the walls.

With the big building boom, developers had been trying to buy the land for years. It was a prime chunk of forest that already separated two big housing developments. But even though her family had moved to California, they'd held on to the property, renting out the house and keeping the land intact. Because while they couldn't live there—the memories were too painful—they didn't want the house leveled and the trees chopped down. And as much as Lucas avoided the place, he was glad it was there, wild and wonderful, with the old trees holding a sort of magic.

His friends were waiting for him. "I'll catch up with you," Lucas called. He watched Josh Duncan swing his backpack over his shoulder. The note felt heavy in his pocket. How could a small slip of paper feel heavy? Lucas wondered. Marvelous Mystery.

The kid slipped out the door. He would follow him. He would give the kid the note but with a warning. He would tell him, "Don't do what it says."

Lucas started to follow and then Mr. K said, "Lucas, can I talk to you for a moment?"

Lucas hesitated. "I'm sort of in a hurry—"

"It will only take a minute." Mr. K came around to the other side of his desk. "I just wanted to check in about Monday. You really all set with your project?"

"Yes," Lucas said, staring straight into his eyes and not blinking.

"And you don't need any help or want to let me know what you'll be presenting about?"

Lucas knew that his best chance for a quick getaway was

to tell Mr. K his topic. Even though he didn't have one. So he blurted it out, the first thing he could think of.

Mr. K sat back and crossed his arms. "Excellent choice. I've always been fascinated by that, too."

"Great—bye—gotta run." Lucas shot for the door.

"See you Monday. I'm looking forward to it."

"Me too," Lucas called back. He ran into the hallway, searching for the very specific color of red. But it was gone. Josh Duncan had, once again, slipped away.

SIBLINGS

Josh sat on Dead Melanie's bench, but he couldn't eat his lunch. He had too many questions to be able to shove food in his mouth and swallow. As far as questions went, these were the biggest:

1. Would he ever find Great-Aunt Evelyn's nephew?
2. Would he ever tell his mom about Big Brother and the sparkly girl?
3. Would he ever see a real banana slug?

He was shivering because of the damp chill in the air, or because of the questions, or because of the proximity to a dormant volcano, or because the pepperoni piled on his plate wouldn't stop staring at him. He peeked around the giant rhododendron bush to see the alien-ship library hovering above the Hello Walk. He couldn't tell his mom, not yet. He would wait until his dad came home—his rational, poster-quoting dad. There would be a perfect inspirational poster for this strange time, and Josh would hang it on his wall, and then—

And then what?

Josh couldn't think that far ahead. When he pulled out his haunted library book, *Land Snails and Slugs of the Pacific Northwest,* Big Brother appeared. He leaned over Josh's shoulder and asked, "Is there really a slug that looks like a banana?"

"Yes," Josh said. "Where have you been?"

"Busy. Any luck finding one?"

"What?"

"A banana slug."

"No. I think you need to go deep into the forest."

"Are you going to do that? Go deep into the forest?"

Josh set his book down. "Are you kidding? There are bears around here. And possibly Bigfoot. It's bad enough just riding my bike next to the forest."

"Fair enough," Big Brother said.

Josh shuffled his feet back and forth. "Sorry. I guess I'm sort of freaking out. It's just—some stuff seems weirder than normal. Even weirder than back when it was weird. Also, did you know a group of crows is called a murder? I forgot to tell you that."

"I didn't know. What else is weird?"

"Well, there's you. You are back. That's sort of weird. I need to tell Mom and Dad about you."

"I know. And you will. When you're ready."

"Yeah, but Mom is weird, too. She's not unpacking the boxes, even though that's what she says she's going to do every day. And her rash is really bad. I don't want to tell her about you until those things are better."

"That's probably smart. So in the meantime, as long as I'm here, I'm still going to give you some big brotherly advice."

"Some more? I liked it better before when we just played games."

Big Brother nodded. "I know. I liked that, too. But we're both older now. And there's something I want you to do. There's a football game tonight. A high school football game. Lots of kids from your school will be going. The whole town will be going—"

"I know. I already heard. It's all people talk about. The Panthers. But how do you know all this?"

"I'm in high school now."

Josh laughed. "Right." He sort of hated Big Brother, but in the normal sibling way that came and went. It had been lonely without him. Sad-monkey lonely. And no one understood him like his brother did.

To change the subject, Josh pointed to his book. "Did you know that banana slugs are the largest slug in North America, probably the second largest slug in the world? They are only found in the western Pacific Northwest coastal lowlands and—"

"What about the game?" Big Brother interrupted.

"I don't like stadiums. What if there's an earthquake? Or a volcanic eruption? Look—" He pulled out his other book from the haunted library and opened to the picture of the blasted mountain. "In 1980, Mount St. Helens blew up. Fifty-seven people were killed."

"That doesn't seem like a lot of people. For a volcano."

"It might seem different if you were one of them."

"Good point, Little Bro. And it's normal to be scared of things. Everyone feels scared of things."

"I don't think that's true."

"It is. And I think that the way you see the world is a good thing."

"What do you mean? The way I see the world?"

"The way you see the gorilla when other people don't—"

"Shut up."

"I mean it. That's a good thing. But it makes it hard sometimes, too."

Josh closed the book. He couldn't look at any more spewing ash and lava. He was close to crying, and he worried that if he started, he wouldn't stop.

"I believe in you, Little Brother."

Josh rubbed his eyes. A few tears had managed to escape.

"If anyone can find a banana slug, it's you."

Josh laughed.

"Tell me something," Big Brother said after a few moments of silence. "Was I right about riding your bike?"

Josh nodded.

"Then I'm right about this, too. You should go tonight. To the game. Sit with kids from your class. See what happens."

Josh wiped his eyes again and cleared his throat and sat up straight and tried to change the subject by telling Big Brother amazing facts about tectonic plates and earthquakes and about Mount Rainier, which at 14,410 feet above sea level, is the highest place in Washington and also considered one of the most dangerous volcanoes in the world. "The world," he added again for emphasis. But Big Brother didn't answer. He was already gone.

LEFTOVERS

There was no way Josh was going to a small-town high school football game. No way ever! Until—leftovers.

Because when he got home and his mom said, "How was your day?" and he said, "Fine. What's for dinner?" and she said, "Leftovers," it didn't sound like leftovers. It sounded like, "Nothing will ever change in your life, not even your dinner. You will be eating meat loaf forever."

Josh went up to his room to kill time before the call-of-doom leftovers. While he waited, he finished sorting the red Lego pieces and got started on the white. Building anything good, like the castle world or the ninja world or the pirate world, would require a trip to the garage and digging through stacks of boxes. It would also require that Josh admit to himself that nothing was as fun as it used to be. Even Lego.

He lay down on his bed. He wished Big Brother would come, but he knew he wouldn't. Even that wasn't the same.

It wasn't yet close to dark, which guaranteed Friday to be the longest night in all of Josh's eleven years. Which meant the longest weekend, too.

He went downstairs.

"Mom," he said, stepping into the kitchen. It was a large kitchen, but suddenly it seemed tiny, like a perfect-fitting sweater that got thrown into a hot dryer.

"Honey? Are you hungry already? Let me just warm up—"

"No, Mom. It's not that."

Josh was pretty sure that if he took one bite of warmed-over food, his heart would stop from the shock of it. It would be like time travel. His body would know he couldn't possibly eat food from the day before because the day before already felt like a hundred years ago. *That* was the problem with the leftovers.

"I'm going out," he said.

"What? Where?"

It was about him not fitting anywhere, even at home. It was about all the secrets he'd been keeping since the move. If he didn't get out, he would explode. No, he would erupt. He was an active volcano.

"Where are you going?" she asked again.

"To a football game," he said, because of Big Brother and because it was the only thing he could think of. "Can you drop me off?"

His mom beamed. "Well, that's wonderful. What time does it start? I'll get my keys. And my warm coat."

"Mom—"

She was all flustered, trying to figure out what to do with the leftovers. She was so happy about going out. "Mom, I was hoping you could just drop me off. At the school. I might meet some people. You know."

"Oh." She stopped.

"If that's okay."

"Of course, honey." She came close and pushed the hair out of his face. "You look different. Older. Maybe it's time for a haircut."

"Mom!" Josh squirmed out of her grasp.

"I trust you to be responsible tonight. I trust you to be careful."

"You can," Josh said. "Trust me. I will be careful and responsible." He couldn't believe it was happening. That he was actually going to a high school football game. And maybe he *would* meet some people—some kids. A friend.

Big Brother had planted that idea, too.

It was one of those things that snowballed. The snowball effect, or in this case, the meat loaf effect. When one small thing starts moving and builds into something bigger until it's an actual big thing—something almost unrecognizable.

GO PANTHERS

After his mom dropped him off at the Mountain View parking lot, Josh took his time crossing the K–8 playfield to the high school stadium.

What

had

he

been

thinking?

Even from the parking lot he could hear the crowd, the band, the cheers. As he passed the dugout, he smelled pine, that Christmas-tree smell, and he felt something new about this place with its quiet roads and damp air. He remembered hiding out on that first day when he ran away from school. Already that seemed like a lifetime ago.

The moon pushed round and bright through the cover of

clouds, and all the stadium lights were turned on, making it seem like a giant campfire on a dark night. Josh let the lights pull him in to the back entrance of the stadium. He remembered it from the tour day with the assistant principal.

There was a ticket booth, with a sign that said STUDENTS— NO CHARGE. Josh walked in and went straight to the back of the stadium, where the concession stands were bright and busy, selling things that smelled extra good, like popcorn and nachos and hot dogs. He watched for a minute, all the color of the crowd, and then followed the line of people balancing their sodas and snacks, up the back steps to the heart of the stadium, where the lights were blinding and the bleachers were packed. For a split second he thought he saw Big Brother standing up in the crowd, next to a girl with long hair. But when Josh blinked, he was gone.

Josh turned his back to the cheering fans and pressed up against the metal railing. Right below him, on the eight-lane track, was a cheer squad of twelve high school girls and boys. There was also a mascot—a person dressed like a panther—and they all danced around and kicked their legs and did things like pyramids and flips.

Josh had never been part of a crowd in that way, and before he knew it, he was stomping his feet with the band and clapping his hands with the cheer squad. He laughed at the funny mascot and cheered for the players as they huddled together and then burst apart. One guy hiked the ball and then everyone ran and crashed and fell and got up and huddled again.

The moon was bright and close—nearly full. Josh smelled that tangy pine again and thought, Somewhere, out there beyond the circle of light, pine trees were standing tall and strong. They were there all the time, even when a person could not see them.

He stayed like that for the whole game, leaning against the railing, smelling pine and cheering with the crowd. When the scoreboard said fourth quarter with two minutes to go, the Panthers were behind by three.

The other team—the Timberwolves—had the ball. The Panthers lined up as the Timberwolf quarterback called out his numbers. The ball shot back into his hands and everyone crashed together. Then, a Panther player broke through the line. He leapt into the air and flew straight at the quarterback.

"AHHHH!" the crowd shouted. But the quarterback stayed calm. He scrambled to his right, kept looking down the field, and finally threw the ball.

Josh admired his calmness in the face of an oncoming player. The ball rose into the sky. It curved and dropped, just as a player from the Timberwolves was positioning himself underneath it, reaching up with open hands.

"AHHHHH!"

The scream came from both sides of the stadium.

"AHHHHH!"

Because right then, a Panther also made a leap. And he tipped the ball, right out of the fingers of the Timberwolf. The ball wobbled in the air as it headed for the ground, but the Panther twisted and stretched even farther and then even farther again.

He actually caught it!

And somehow, when it looked like he would fall flat on his face, he broke the law of gravity. He didn't fall. He held on to the ball and landed on his feet and spun around and, as the crowd started to roar, he thundered down the field.

He was at the fifty-yard line.

The forty.

The thirty.

When he got to the twenty, Josh started to jump, just like the rest of the crowd. They jumped. They screamed. They jumped and screamed to help their very own Panther make the touchdown.

And he did!

He crossed into the end zone and the stands erupted. When Josh spun around to look at the stadium, his arms shot straight up. And that's when he understood why people went to games and screamed until their voices cracked. The players out there—they were his dad's inspirational posters, come to life.

"YEAAAAH!" he screamed with the rest of them. Bodies hugged and jumped and danced to the music. The biggest celebration ever was happening all around Josh. And he was a part of it. He was finally in the movie he'd always wanted to be in.

Down below on the track, the cheer squad was making a giant pyramid. They were making a giant pyramid, just like in the movies. He saw a flash of red. The pyramid was done and the crowd was doing some sort of chant with the cheerleaders . . . *Who are we? Pan-thers* . . . and then at the base of the human pyramid, one more person began to crawl to the top. Josh leaned forward. No, it couldn't be.

Yes, it was.

Great-Aunt Evelyn. In her red tracksuit. Stepping onto shoulders and elbows and heads. Grabbing with her gnarled oak-tree hands.

When she reached the top of the pyramid, she wobbled to her feet and balanced there, on the shoulders of the top smiling cheerleader. She raised her arms and stared across the track.

"Did you find my Jackie?" Josh saw her mouth moving and heard her voice in his ear. He was pinned against the railing, staring straight across to the top of the pyramid into Great-Aunt Evelyn's watery blue eyes.

"Do you still have the book?"

Josh thought she might go away if he showed her the Robert Frost poetry book. He maneuvered his backpack to his front and unzipped the top. He pulled out the book and held it up, but by then the pyramid had disassembled and Great-Aunt Evelyn was on the ground, kicking her leg. It looked, alarmingly, like she was getting ready to do a cartwheel.

"Hey!" Josh called and waved the book to get her attention. But a push from behind sent the book flying out of his hands.

"No!" Josh yelled. The book landed on the track, splayed out and open. He frantically looked around. How to get down there? The crowd was pushing even harder, pinning him to the rail. Then he felt a hand on his shoulder. He turned his head. It was a kid Josh recognized from Mr. K's class. Lucas Hernandez.

Josh opened his mouth and tried to explain. "My book!" He pointed.

The kid pressed up next to his shoulder and looked down at the track. "Here," he said. "Follow me."

And he pushed through the crowd, making space for Josh to follow.

TOUCHDOWN

If there was one thing that could take Lucas Hernandez's mind off his problems, it was a football game. Especially a Panthers football game.

Lucas loved the high school games. He loved how the air was crisp, and the lights were bright. He loved the large rectangle of green field divided by neat white lines. He loved the end zones and the music and the nachos he always shared with his friends. He loved it all.

His cousin had just made the most amazing game-winning interception and the band was playing "Louie Louie" and he and his friends were dancing, when he saw her. Down against the railing. In her sparkly shirt. Pointing at Josh Duncan in his bright red raincoat.

Lucas groaned.

The cheer squad was in a pyramid by the time he'd stepped

over legs and pushed past shoulders. His friends, he was sure, hadn't noticed that he'd slipped away. He would meet up with them later, at Dairy Queen. First he would give the kid the stupid note so that everything could go back to normal.

Maxie Moon was nowhere in sight, but that didn't matter. Lucas reached the railing and touched the kid on the shoulder. "Excuse me—" he started, but Josh Duncan spun around with the most panicked look on a face that Lucas had ever seen.

"Sorry—" Lucas said.

"My book!" Josh Duncan pointed over the railing.

Lucas leaned over and saw a small book lying on the track. He felt bad for the kid. "Here," he said. "Follow me." He led Josh through the crowd, weaving around bodies and pushing against the oncoming mass of people. It made him think about how salmon battled to swim upstream, to spawn in the same place they had hatched. It was a Marvelous Mystery for sure.

"Almost there," he called, and glanced back to make sure the kid was still right behind him. Then he ran down the length of the backside of the stadium, past overflowing garbage cans and the little kids playing football with an invisible ball.

A security guard stood between the back of the stadium and the entrance to the field. "He dropped his book," Lucas explained. The guard nodded and moved aside.

It could have been fun, Lucas thought, as his feet hit the

springy track. With the lights all around and half the crowd still in the stands, it could have been fun. But Maxie Moon was at the railing again, looking down at him, making sure he did what he had promised to do.

As Josh Duncan ran to retrieve the book, Lucas reached into his pocket and took out the note. He would hand it to him and say, "Ignore this. Don't do what it says. I just have to hand it to you. It's like—a dare. For me. Don't even read it."

That's how he'd do it.

And then maybe he'd invite the kid to Dairy Queen.

Josh Duncan had picked up the book but was just standing there, slumped, like something was wrong. Lucas walked over with the note in his hand.

"There was money," Josh said. "In the book. I need to find it." He handed Lucas the book and started searching the track.

Lucas looked down, first at the book of poems, and then around the ground. He spotted a fluttery piece of paper, about to blow onto the field. "There!" he called, and pointed.

Josh ran after it clumsily and Lucas remembered the first time he'd seen the kid, running between the buildings in the same red raincoat but with an inexplicable shadow.

He shivered.

And then he did it. Something sneaky. Something that wasn't part of the plan.

Josh ran back with a wide-open grin. He stopped in front of Lucas and looked down at his feet. "Thankyousomuch!"

"No problem." The way Lucas handed Josh the book of poems was as smooth as a perfectly executed play. If they'd been playing football, it would have led to a touchdown.

When he turned and walked away there were two things he would regret almost instantly:

1. He didn't invite Josh Duncan to Dairy Queen.
2. He slipped the note into the book of poetry.

TWO SHADOWS

Josh crossed the playfield and went straight to the spot where his mom had arranged to pick him up. The moon, so bright earlier in the night, was now tucked behind the clouds. Groups of kids were all around, talking and laughing, and still excited about the game. Like Josh, many of them were waiting for rides. But they were waiting for rides together. So he stood there, waiting for his mom, and all that darkness and dampness and *aloneness* made him feel like he was, once again, lost at sea without an anchor.

Then his anchor appeared. Josh felt him before he saw him. He looked around and saw a shadow. Two shadows? "Hey!" he said. "Where have you been?"

"What do you mean?" Big Brother acted surprised.

Josh shook his head. This was all so different from when

he was younger and the only thing they fought about was whether to build a Lego space station or medieval fortress.

"I thought I saw you. At the game. Up in the stands. But you were with someone. And then you were gone."

"Great game, wasn't it? Could you believe that ending?"

Josh nodded. In all that had just happened, with the book and Lucas Hernandez and Great-Aunt Evelyn, he'd nearly forgotten the magical moment, when the ball was flying, and he was part of the crowd. "Yeah," he said. "It was great."

"And you did it—you went to your very first football game! Did you have fun?"

"I guess. But I blew it again."

"What did you blow? What happened?"

Josh didn't want to explain how Lucas Hernandez had been so nice, so helpful. And then, when Josh couldn't even talk to him, well—no wonder the kid wanted to get away from him so fast.

"What happened?" Big Brother asked again.

Josh erupted. "Why can't I talk like a normal person? Why do I get so nervous?"

"Hey, hey, hey," Big Brother said softly. "That's not how I see it at all."

"Well then, you aren't—" Josh stopped himself. He didn't even know, really, what he was about to say. He knew he wanted to say something hurtful. Something to put Big Brother in his place and to get him to shut his Big Brother mouth.

What he didn't want was a pep talk. He didn't want someone who wasn't even part of the world telling him how to think and feel and act in the world.

Big Brother waited a moment. Then he said, "I'll tell you what I saw tonight. I saw a brave kid. The bravest. I saw how you showed up. Alone. How you put yourself out there. And I was proud of you. So proud."

Josh knew that Big Brother meant it. But he had his own truth. "When Lucas Hernandez ran away like that—"

"You thought that was about you?"

"Well, yeah. Of course."

"Do you want some big brotherly advice?"

"You're going to give it to me, whether I want it or not."

"You don't always know what's going on with a person. You might think it's all about you. But maybe it's about them. Maybe, maybe . . ."

"Maybe you need to go lie down in a dirt hole again." The terrible words were out before Josh could stop them. And he didn't mean them, not at all. The moment they left his mouth he wanted to take them back. He wanted to say he was sorry, so sorry, and that he never wanted Big Brother to go away again. Ever.

All those words wanted to come out, but his mouth would not open to let them. In the silence, Josh heard noises around him. They'd been there all along, the talking and laughing of friends. He glanced over. The shadow of Big Brother was there, but it didn't feel like it.

"Maybe you need to talk to Mom," Big Brother said finally, quietly.

Josh wanted to say how sorry he was, but the words didn't come. He saw the headlights of his mom's car, and her worried face in the lights of the parking lot, seeking him out.

"See you around, Bro," his big brother said, slipping off into the night.

When Josh opened the car door, his mother looked past him. He heard her catch her breath. For a moment it seemed as though she was seeing something.

"Mom?"

Her eyes blinked. She shook her head. "The stadium looks so pretty like that."

She said it softly, almost sadly. But when Josh slid into the front seat and she asked, "How was the game?" her voice was back to normal.

"It was fine." Josh rested his forehead on the cold glass window. "We won."

He watched the shadow of Big Brother walk back across

the field. Next to him was another shadow. There were two shadows walking side by side, into the night.

He remembered what Big Brother had said. *You don't always know what's going on with a person. You might think it's all about you. But maybe it's about them.*

"I'm sorry," Josh whispered, even though it felt like it was too late.

"What?" his mother asked sharply.

"I said, we won." Then the car turned the corner and the two shadows were out of sight.

MISTAKES

The thing about mistakes, Lucas told himself, was you often had a chance to fix them. That's what his mom always said. And like in Mr. K's class, when you messed up on a test, you could do corrections. Some mistakes you couldn't fix, as Lucas knew all too well. Some were permanent. It was a hard fact to live with.

Lucas was still feeling bad about his latest mistake with the new kid. He was in bed but he couldn't sleep from thinking about it. Or maybe it was because he'd eaten a DQ Blizzard after his large chocolate-dipped cone. He rolled over. His stomach hurt and his head hurt. The head was from Josh Duncan. How he'd slipped the note into his book, without explanation or warning. Then he left him there, all alone out on the track. But most of all, his head was worried about what might happen the next day. Saturday. If Josh Duncan found the note.

How often does a kid open a book of poetry? That was the big question. But the fact that he was reading it at a football game—a Panthers game!—made Lucas think there was a good chance he would open the book and find it. And then what? Would he follow the note's instructions?

Maybe he wouldn't realize the note was intended for him. Lucas almost talked himself into believing that. But if he did actually follow the map and go to the house? It wouldn't be Lucas's fault. Not—at—all.

That was the other thing about mistakes. You could talk yourself out of thinking you made one.

SEISMIC

When Josh woke early Saturday morning, he pulled the covers over his head and tried to go back to sleep. But the bright sun coming through the window wouldn't let him. Downstairs, his mom was at the kitchen counter, hunched over the newspaper with a cup of coffee. She straightened when Josh walked in. "So! What are your weekend plans?"

"Homework," Josh said. "What are yours?"

She motioned to the boxes. She scratched her wrist.

Josh ate his breakfast and went outside. The ground was still wet from the night before, and the sun made everything sparkle. He popped his head back in and told his mom he was going for a bike ride. "Not too far," she said.

He took out his bike and rode it around the circular drive. He was hungry again, but he didn't want to go back in and see his mom staring at boxes and old photographs. The weekend seemed too long already.

What would Big Brother tell him to do? When the answer came to him, he turned off the circular drive and headed for the main road.

He could ride anywhere. He had five dollars in his backpack, left over from the money his mom had given him for the football game, and he could pedal the short distance into town and get something to eat. By himself.

He knew he had Big Brother to thank for his newfound independence, and it gave him an ache, deep in his chest, to think about the terrible things he said after the football game. He tried his best to push the conversation out of his mind, along with the image of the two shadows walking off into the night.

The Last Stop was open, and the sign still said corn dogs, two for one. Josh turned in and leaned his bike against the side of the building. When he opened the door, he heard the bell tinkle and remembered the first time, when he'd run away from school. It felt so long ago, but it wasn't really. Not in regular time, anyway. But in a different kind of time, it was something like years. Did the invisible crack make that happen, too? Make time change into something else?

The man at the counter greeted him, and Josh greeted

him back. That small exchange made him think about all the rules that were part of living in the world. He would walk into a store and pick up something and give the person behind the counter green paper or shiny coins, and then he could leave.

This is what Josh was thinking as he set his PayDay on the counter and asked the man for a corn dog. They were extra brown, probably left over from the night before.

"Two for one," the man said.

"Okay," Josh said. "I'll take two." He glanced down the counter at the bundles of wood, the Zippo lighters, and the sign that advertised worms. He remembered that first day, when he'd dreamed of running away to live on the mountain. It made him think of something, but he didn't know exactly what.

He tucked the PayDay in his backpack but held both corn dogs in one hand, by the warm sticks, and he walked out and sat on the curb to eat them. Even though it was a convenience store parking lot and he was sitting next to an overflowing garbage can, the air smelled like it had been washed clean with rainwater and pine needles. A breeze swept across a puddle of water near his feet, and he saw a rainbow shimmer in the middle of it. The corn dogs were good—crunchy and sweet on the outside and steamy in the middle.

On the way home, belly full of one corn dog too many,

Josh realized what it was—the thing he was trying to understand when he was looking at the bundles of wood, the Zippo lighters, and the worm sign.

The world was shifting beneath him. It was a fact. Seismic events were happening at the very core of the earth—things he couldn't always feel or see but he knew they were there.

The thing he was trying to think of in the store—it was that he was shifting, too. He wasn't the same kid who had run away from his first day of school. He was now a kid who rode his bike and went to high school football games and ordered convenience store corn dogs when he was hungry. Those were big changes and Big Brother had made them happen. Josh knew that. He also knew something big was shifting in their relationship. He couldn't explain it because he didn't understand it. And it wasn't like an earthquake, something he could feel. It was more that he could see the aftereffects. The jumble of ruins.

He found his mom in the living room surrounded by photos. Her face was blotchy and red. "Are you hungry?" she asked, wiping her eyes.

Josh told her he'd gone to the store. She raised her eyebrows, like she had something to say, but nothing came out.

"I'm going upstairs," Josh said. "Homework."

"I almost forgot—your dad called. I told him you went to the game last night. He wants you to call him."

Josh had an okay talk with his dad. At the end, though, his dad said a bunch of things like "Hang in" and "Good job" and "Go get 'em." Josh could tell he was all choked up with genuine fatherly happiness, which made him feel like even more of a big awful liar.

He took out some Lego but it wasn't fun. It was barely past noon and the day was dragging on. It was so boring that he looked forward to doing his homework.

He opened his backpack and took out the books from the old library. When he saw the Robert Frost poems, he thought about the night before. He'd been trying so hard not to think about it, but there it was—right before him.

Great-Aunt Evelyn.

Lucas Hernandez.

The fact that he would never make a friend.

He opened the book to see her shaky inscription again: *To my wonderful nephew, Jackie. Happy Birthday. With Buckets of Love from Great-Aunt Evelyn.*

A piece of paper fell out. He unfolded it. It was a note. The world shifted again.

THE NOTE

Gorilla Club
Saturday at Sundown
Follow the Map
Find Your Way In

Josh couldn't make sense of what he was reading. He remembered the girl who had said the words *Gorilla Club*. Of course he remembered her. She'd tapped her toes and told him about Dead Melanie's bench—that Melanie had been run over while crossing the street in the middle of the day. She'd held up her hand and announced, "First meeting of the Gorilla Club." Josh remembered it all.

But it wasn't real. She wasn't part of the world that he was a part of. Except—there was a note. Paper and pen. Things that *were* of this world.

Gorilla Club. Find your way in.

The note made it real.

THE HOUSE
IN THE WOODS

It used to be called the Cascalenda house, which was the name of the immigrant family from Italy who had cleared the bit of land and built a home with their own timber and hands. Years later, when the developers began to arrive with contracts and checkbooks, the Cascalendas were the one family in the area that held out. They held on to their land.

Back when they first moved to this remote forest, they grew food and raised animals—chickens and rabbits and pigs. They got jobs with the nearby timber company. The large family house was passed down to a new generation, and then another. One of the Cascalenda daughters got married and changed her last name to her husband's last name, which was Moon. All around them, houses and local schools were built. Even when the name on the mailbox was Moon, some people still thought of it as the old Cascalenda house.

Until the terrible thing happened and it became known simply as the House in the Woods.

The Moons had one child, a girl, who was the Apple of Everyone's Eye. That's what they said, all the time. "Maxie Moon, you are the apple of our eye." She never knew what that meant but she knew it was good. She imagined one giant and adoring eye, directed at her at all times.

She was tiny but full of energy. When her grandmother came to live with them, the two became great friends. Maxie loved her nonna with all her heart. Nonna taught her Italian words and fried up slices of salami and green peppers because that was Maxie's favorite. She taught her granddaughter how to dance, too, swirling her around the kitchen table. "I never knew a time when I couldn't cook or couldn't dance," she told Maxie, adding sounds to her words that no one else did.

The area was growing. Every year, a developer would approach with a new deal. "Your land is in the way of our plans." Or, "We need to build a road and you'll have to move."

But the Cascalenda-Moon family didn't budge. Like giant hands dropping cookie cutters into the forest, the developers carved out the land. Except for the Cascalenda house. The house in the woods.

And then came the tragedy. But even after that, they stood

firm on one thing: The house and land would remain. How could it not? Their beloved child would always be there.

Lucas knew the house was still there. He knew because of the real estate agents that passed through and the FOR RENT notices and the moving trucks that came in with new families and then left not too long after.

He knew because of the stories they told, as they moved to another house, a house in Hidden Peaks or Silver Pines or Cougar Ridge or any one of the other developments. The stories were mostly the same.

Doors that slammed in the middle of the night.

Sounds of crying from the upstairs closet.

A smell of smoke that just wouldn't go away.

No one had stayed for an entire year. Most left after a few months. With every new family, the people who remembered held their breath. Maybe it would be different this time? Maybe the story would end? The house had been empty nearly two years—the longest stretch since it happened. Fences had gone up and NO TRESPASSING signs. Still, the Moon family was not about to sell it. Ever.

On Saturday morning when Lucas woke up, he didn't just roll out of bed as usual. He bolted upright. Had he been dreaming about the house? The house in the woods?

He knew what day it was. It was a date he didn't like to

think about, not ever. But especially not on this particular Saturday, because of the note. And because of that kid, Josh Duncan.

He dragged out of bed and went downstairs. His dad was outside doing something in the yard, his mom in the shower, and his little sisters were playing checkers at the kitchen table. When he poured himself a bowl of Cheerios, they asked for bowls, too.

"Are you coming to our soccer game?" they asked at the exact same time.

Lucas told them that he couldn't since he had to finish his Marvelous Mysteries project. "But I will next week." They made him pinkie promise.

Twins, he thought. *My sisters are a Marvelous Mystery.*

He set down their bowls of cereal and said, "If you had to ask one big question about the world, the biggest mystery ever, what would it be?"

Isabel said, "Where can I find a unicorn?"

Ava said, "Why can't we get a dog?"

Lucas took out his Marvelous Mysteries brainstorm sheet and pretended to write both down. His sisters giggled.

Then Isabel said, "How about the house in the woods?"

Lucas felt his heart speed up. He stared at the bright yellow box of cereal and took a deep breath. "Who told you anything about that?"

"Everyone talks about it at school."

"Those are just a bunch of stories." He tried to keep his voice light. "There's nothing interesting there. So just—stay away from it, okay?"

OLD SPICE
AND NAILS

As the day dragged on, Josh Duncan thought about the note. He carried it in his pocket so he could read it, over and over. It seemed like something alive, something that required attention and tending. No, that wasn't it. Not exactly.

It was heavy. That's what. But paper couldn't be heavy, could it? Josh eventually slipped the note back in the book of Robert Frost poems, as he'd found it. He left the book in his room. He even closed the door.

When he went downstairs, he found his mom in the living room, pulling more photos out of boxes, ones he'd never seen before. "More photos?" he asked.

"I thought about what you said. About setting everything back in the same place. I thought we could line these up on the wall next to the stairs. That would be different." She pushed the hair away from her face. "But I think we need more nails. How about a trip to the hardware store?"

Josh rode along, staring out the window, wishing the ride would last all day. More than anything, he wanted to keep busy. If he just kept busy enough, he thought, he'd be able to stop thinking about the note. And the house in the woods. And Big Brother.

In the hardware store on Main Street, his mom pulled down the biggest box of nails she could find. Josh tried to make a joke. "Are we building a new house?"

His mom laughed with him. "It's cheaper to buy in bulk." But her rash was covering her hand, and she was walking too fast.

The minute they got home Josh dashed upstairs and read the note again. He went through the checklist of what he knew. The note was real, that was the main thing. So even though the sparkly girl had been the one to use the words *Gorilla Club*, someone real had actually written the note.

The girl had also mentioned Lucas Hernandez as the one other kid in Mr. K's class who had seen the gorilla in the video. And—Lucas Hernandez was the one who had helped Josh reclaim his book and the ten dollars at the football game. He was the only other person who had held the book in his hands. So, maybe it was real. And maybe there would be a meeting. In a house. In the woods. At sundown.

Josh paced his room. He studied the map. Because of the time he'd spent on his bike, he knew exactly where the map was directing him—to the edge of the Bear Creek development, where the new houses were being built. And then, the trail into the woods.

His mom was hammering nails into the smooth taupe walls. The house was shaking from her pounding. She was hanging pictures he'd never seen before. Every time she pounded another nail with her rash-covered hand, he remembered. All the family photographs she wanted to hang made him think about his big brother, the only one he would ever have. He remembered the awful words he'd said to him. He remembered how he'd walked off into the night, like a shadow.

Josh grabbed his backpack and shoved in the book of poetry and the note. He was sweating in his armpits again, so he went to the bathroom and searched through the cabinet of his parents' weird stuff until he found what he was looking for. He took off the lid and sniffed. The smell was strong and confident and reminded Josh of his dad. He missed him right then, but he was also glad he was not there for the moment that Josh rubbed the deodorant on his underarms and transformed into a grown-up lumberjack.

Josh squared his backpack and marched down the stairs. As he squeezed past his hammering mom, he glanced at a photo of his six-year-old self in a pumpkin patch. He remembered the day: Big Brother had been there, too. He'd pointed out the best pumpkin for him to pick.

"Where are you going, Josh?"

"To a friend's house," he said, which wasn't exactly a lie. "I joined a club at school. We have a meeting."

His mom followed him down the stairs, sniffing. "I smell something. Old Spice. Did you use your dad's deodorant?"

"Well, yeah," Josh admitted. "Sorry—"

"No, no, that's perfectly fine. I'll buy you your own—"

"That's okay." Josh and his mom stood there awkwardly, the smell of Old Spice filling the air with something new. "Well . . . ," he started.

"What time will you be home?"

"I don't know." He didn't know. He had no idea.

"You're really growing up. Riding your bike to school. Joining clubs. Going to high school football games—"

"Well, not—"

"I was going through a box of your old baby stuff—" She stopped talking. Her eyes filled with tears.

"Okay, Mom. I should go. I can't be late for the meeting."

She nodded and wiped her face. "What do you want for dinner tonight? Would you like pizza? I found a place that delivers."

"Actually I don't know how late I'll be." That was true. Not a lie. "I'll probably stay there for dinner."

She was still nodding. "So what kind of club is this?"

"It's sort of a science club. With some kids from my class."

"That's wonderful. How about I drop you off?"

"That's okay. I'll ride my bike. It's really close to our house."

"But what if it's dark when you're done?"

"Then I'll call and you can pick me up. Or I can get a ride home."

His mom came close. "I knew this move would be good. I knew you would—" And then she sort of crumpled. Josh didn't know how else to describe it. She sort of fell over herself and started to cry. At first he didn't know she was crying because no sounds were coming out.

"Mom?" Josh was alarmed. "Are you okay? Do you want me to call Dad?"

"No, don't call your father. Don't worry." She wiped her cheeks with the back of her hand. "I'm okay, honey. I just haven't looked at this stuff in such a long time. Really looked at it, you know. And these photos of you as a baby—" She raised her hands helplessly. "I just love you so much. You know? And suddenly, here you are, smelling like Old Spice."

Josh nodded. Only he didn't have any idea what she was talking about. He thought it had something to do with the move and the boxes she had to unpack. He glanced again at the wall. So many nails. So many pictures. It was too much to take in, so Josh studied the details.

The button on the back of a chair.

The way the lampshade was tilted half an inch.

This perfectly round mark on the coffee table, the shape of the bottom of a cup. All things that told him these moments frozen in time—they had been real.

His mom stood close, watching him. "If it gets dark I don't want you riding home. Promise?"

Josh held up his hand like a Boy Scout. "I promise." And as he lowered his hand, he made a silent vow. No more lies. After this one night he would come clean about everything: the alien-ship library; Great-Aunt Evelyn; the sparkly girl; and everything else. Especially Big Brother. After this night. He gave his mom a tight hug and went to the garage for his bike.

When he was halfway down the driveway, he heard the hammer start up again.

STONEHENGE

After class on Friday, when Mr. K had pulled Lucas aside to ask what topic he'd chosen for his Marvelous Mystery presentation, Lucas had blurted out the first thing that came to mind.

"Stonehenge! I'm doing it on Stonehenge."

Lucas had always been interested in Stonehenge. When he was younger, he used to collect rocks and make tiny replicas of the circle of stacked stones. He and Maxie would do it together. That hadn't occurred to him, when he'd blurted out the word to Mr. K. The very last thing he wanted was one more thing that made him think about Maxie Moon, but it was too late to do anything about it.

When his sisters were off to their soccer game and the house was quiet, Lucas settled at the table with the research books he'd checked out from the media center. He started by writing a tidy introductory paragraph.

Stonehenge is a prehistoric monument and one of the most famous landmarks in the United Kingdom. It is in Wiltshire, England, and people come from all over the world to see it. It is a group of standing stones and archaeologists think it was put together around 3000 BC. No one really knows what Stonehenge is, or how it came to be. Some people think it's a burial ground. Some people think aliens built it. It is a (marvelous) mystery.

He stopped. The words were flat, the paper was flat. There was not a bit of magic or mystery in any of it. What if, instead of writing a paper, he made a replica, with rocks, the way he and Maxie used to?

For the very first time Lucas felt a spark of excitement about his project. He took out a fresh sheet of paper and began to sketch, using the photo in his book as a guide. When he was finished, he grabbed a grocery bag from the pantry and went out to collect rocks.

He found himself heading for the strip of forest between his development and the next one over, Bear Creek. It was where he and Maxie Moon used to look for rocks, when they were playing at his house. Most times, though, they played at hers. Her house in the woods.

It made him remember.

They'd met on the first day of kindergarten. Lucas and his family had just moved from the city and because he was new and hadn't gone to preschool with anyone, he was shy in class. She came up to him right away on the playground and smiled with her whole mouth open. He was impressed because she was missing a tooth. In circle time the teacher had asked, "Maxie, did the tooth fairy visit you?"

"The tooth fairy doesn't come if your tooth gets knocked out by a soccer ball," she answered, grinning. "That's what Nonna said."

Her big grin and missing tooth made her look older and slightly creepy, but in a good way. She and Lucas played together all that day, and then his mom got a call from her mom. "All she talks about is Lucas Hernandez! We'd love to have him over to play."

There was a road, of course, but the kids soon discovered the shortcut trail just behind the Bear Creek Development and through the woods. They were back and forth on it several times a day.

Lucas wasn't shy with Maxie like he was with other kids. They took turns deciding what to play. Maxie liked running and climbing. Lucas liked hunting for rocks and digging for treasure. It was always fun, no matter what they did, and Lucas felt he was at home in Maxie's house.

Now, bent over to pick up a rock, Lucas froze. Why was he thinking about all this today? He'd given the note to Josh Duncan so Maxie would go away and leave him alone, forever. Because that's what he'd wanted, more than anything. But here he was, suddenly thinking about all that stuff—her smile, her grandmother, the games they used to play. All the stuff he'd tried to forget about, ever since the accident.

He dropped the rock into his bag and moved to find another one. He worked fast and tried to concentrate on the task, but he couldn't stop the images that crept back into his head. He saw fog. Or was it smoke? He saw the small grave. He heard the sound of wailing from the funeral. The horrible sound.

It was this day, in the fall of first grade.

A gorilla stepped into the circle and beat its chest. No one saw. No one but the new kid. The kid who now had the note.

Without noticing, Lucas had filled his sack so full of rocks it was almost too heavy to carry. He dragged it back home across the forest floor, and then across the driveway, and then the neatly mown lawn. On the porch, he fumbled with the bag and the doorknob, and once inside, he noticed how very quiet the house was.

He wished he'd gone to the soccer game with his sisters and mom and dad. After the game they were going to their uncle's birthday party, which would last all day and into the evening. He'd begged his parents to let him stay home. "I need to finish this before Monday," he'd explained. "And I haven't even started."

They had finally agreed. Now he wondered, what had he been thinking? An entire day alone? And on this day—of all days? He guessed his parents had forgotten, or if they remembered, they must have hoped he had forgotten.

Lucas found the glue. He spread out an old newspaper and arranged the rocks on the kitchen table, looking for shapes and smooth surfaces that were similar to the ones in his book. Each rock was just a rock, on its own. But when they began to pile up, that's when the magic happened.

The rocks worked their magic on Lucas, and he found himself absorbed by the task. Rocks! Even just holding an ordinary-looking gray stone made him feel close to something ancient and magical, and made him remember that the world was full of one marvelous mystery after another.

He was nearly done with the second column. He sat back to look at what he'd done. With all the rocks he'd collected, he seemed to be missing a certain shape, so he put the second column aside and started on the third.

The phone rang and he jumped. He looked out the window to the darkened sky. He answered the phone and talked to his mom. She told him the party was fun and everyone missed him. "Everything okay? You getting your project done?"

"Still working on it," he said, and they talked a little more. After he hung up he realized he was hungry, so he pulled out a large mixing bowl and filled it with the rest of the Cheerios. He dumped in milk and settled back down to puzzle out his rocks. He wondered if the twins had won their soccer game.

The tooth fairy doesn't come if you get your tooth knocked out by a soccer ball.

Lucas hunkered down and studied the Stonehenge photo. He separated his rocks. He would need another shape to make it work.

Where can I find a unicorn?

Why can't we get a dog?

How about the house in the woods?

He slurped the last of his milk and rinsed out the bowl. He would go looking for the rock he needed, before it got dark. He turned on the kitchen light, and then went through the house and turned on all the lights. The house seemed so quiet. Why didn't he go with them? Why did he stay here alone?

Lucas slipped on a sweatshirt. He would have to find just the right rock. Maybe he'd have to venture a bit deeper since he'd scoured his patch of woods pretty clean. He pushed away troubling thoughts as he walked down the hall, thoughts of the note and the kid and the day it was.

He opened the front door and then he stopped. Right in

the center of the welcome mat was a rock. A perfect rock. The exact rock he needed for his Stonehenge project.

He knew he must have dropped it earlier, when he'd been fumbling at the door with his heavy bag. He believed that. But he also believed it was something more. He believed the rock carried a message, just for him. He believed that because the moment he saw it, right there on the welcome mat, he knew what he had to do.

LOSER TOUCHES THE HOUSE

Josh rode past the skeleton houses and the dirt mounds, all the way to the giant evergreen tree where the obstacle-course kids had pointed out the entrance to the trail. Along with the NO TRESPASSING sign, a barbed-wire fence gave the clear message to stay away.

Josh got off his bike and leaned it against the tree. Then he stepped close to the fence and peered down the path. It was so dark with overgrown branches he couldn't see very far in. Plus—he looked at the sky. The sun was going down. It would be dark soon.

He wished there was a poster that said *Halfway, and you've gone far enough.* Or, *Always listen to the barbed-wire fence.* He also wished Big Brother would appear and say, Good job, Josh. Let's go home and build a city with Legos.

Josh didn't get those wishes. But he did get something.

He remembered Big Brother's words, on the second first day of school. He took a deep breath. "Okay, Big Brother. Life is a glorious adventure, or it is nothing."

It wasn't only Big Brother's words that made Josh step up to the fence. It wasn't the grown-up smell of Old Spice deodorant, either. Those helped, but Josh continued moving forward because, for the first time in a long time, he had a place to go. A place where someone—someone real and of this world—might be waiting for him.

Carefully he positioned his hands between the sharp barbs and put his foot on the lowest wire. The fence swayed and sagged but held him.

The next step was harder. The wire wobbled and Josh clutched at the wooden post. At the top, he swung his first leg over. But when he shifted his weight and tried to swing the other, he lost his balance. He tipped and fell—all the way to the ground.

Josh lay still for a moment, assessing the damage. His hands were scraped. His chin felt bruised. When he looked up at the fence he saw a piece of his new red raincoat, stuck to the barbed wire like a sad flapping flag. But when he got to his feet and brushed himself off, he felt sort of like a champion. Or at least how he imagined a champion might feel. Because he'd fallen, but to the other side. He'd made it. Buoyed by that feeling of success, Josh started down the path.

Leaves rustled, twigs snapped, trees crowded, and a crow swooped so close to his head that it blew back his hair. The trail was damp and his pants were soon wet up to his knees. Rotting smells filled his nose. But he kept going.

The trail through the dark forest was longer than it had looked on the hand-drawn map. Josh was relieved when the path intersected something that looked like a driveway. He continued on the driveway until the forest opened up to a large, unkempt yard and a house tucked far back into the trees. Josh remembered the obstacle-course kids as he took it all in—the mess of overgrown grass, weeds, and brambles.

Loser touches the house.

The house was two floors of sagging wood, peeling paint, and boarded-up windows with shards of broken glass. There was a long front porch with an old broken chair. This couldn't be it. Could it? As he stood there, a wispy fog crept in from the forest. A crow circled above his head. Josh glanced at the crow, the fog, and the darkening sky. He turned back to the house. "Hello?" he called.

Only the crow answered.

He took a step back and tripped over a patch of weeds. Stunned, he lay on his back as the wind whipped up, sending the giant pine trees swaying in their slow-motion silent laughter. His chest squeezed tight. His backpack was pinned underneath him.

He thought, *This maybe wasn't the best idea in the world.*

The crow screeched again. Josh watched it dive from the highest branch of a swaying pine straight to the rooftop of the old abandoned house. And that's when he saw the thing that made his heart nearly explode. Movement. In the upstairs window.

It was a face, in the shadows, looking down on him. Like it had been waiting.

ROCK

After Lucas discovered the rock on the front-porch welcome mat, he went straight to his room. He rarely opened his closet door, even for clothes. He preferred to keep his clothes in the dresser, or piled on his floor, because he didn't even like looking at the closed closet door. But when he went to his room he went straight to his closet and opened the door. He held his breath as he stepped into the dark space—all the way to the darkest corner of the dark space, where he grabbed a dusty old shoebox.

Clutching it tightly, he ran down the stairs. His hand was on the front doorknob when he remembered to leave his parents a note. So he ran back to the kitchen and grabbed a pen and scribbled something about helping a friend, which wasn't exactly a lie. He wrote that he'd be back later, not sure when, but he would call if it was too late or dark or whatever (he didn't actually know what he was saying at that point, but he wanted them to know he would be safe, even though, of course, he had no idea how unsafe the night could get).

He opened the front door and stepped over the rock on the welcome mat. Then he turned back and picked it up. He slipped it in his pocket, grabbed his bike, and pedaled fast for the place he told himself he would never go again.

The sun was about to go down. If Josh Duncan showed up at the house, Lucas would be there first. He would be there to warn him away. He had to. The rock had reminded him of all the things he'd tried to forget.

Even though Lucas hadn't been on that route for years, he still knew every twist and turn of the trail, and every stump and mossy boulder next to it. Holding the box in one arm, he rode across to the next housing development, Bear Creek, and came to the newest construction site.

A NO TRESPASSING sign had been posted in front of the entrance to the trail into the woods, and a barbed-wire fence had been installed. Leaning up against a tree was a bike. But it looked too small to belong to Josh Duncan. Plus, it was bright yellow with SpongeBob all over it. He put his own bike next to it and climbed the fence. As he was hopping down, something caught his eye. He bent closer. Stuck to one of the barbs was a torn piece of red fabric—the exact color of the kid's enormous raincoat. Lucas started to run.

THE HOLE

Josh was in a hole. Not a symbolic one, but a real hole. And sitting there in the hole, nothing made sense.

Before the hole, he'd been looking for a way in. First, he'd stepped onto the sagging front porch with the old broken chair and knocked on the boarded-up door. As he was knocking, he came to realize that even if someone did want to open the door, the nailed-in boards wouldn't let them.

Back in the tall weeds in the middle of the yard, Josh studied the upstairs window. *Find your way in.* The note had said it.

The watchful crow launched off the rooftop. It landed close to him and began to hop. Not toward Josh, but in the opposite direction—toward the house.

As it neared the side of the house, Josh had a strange thought. Why, he wondered, was the crow hopping instead of flying? Did it want Josh to follow?

It seemed impossibly preposterous, but was it any more than any of it?

Still as the crow hopped away, Josh stayed where he was, in the middle of the yard. The moon was just coming up from behind the line of trees—full and round and bright. A dark shadow crossed it, and then another. Josh watched as shadow after shadow crossed in front of the full moon and landed on the tall swaying pine.

That was it.

What had seemed like a good idea earlier, when his mom had been pounding millions of nails into the wall, now seemed really stupid. Josh imagined what he must look like, standing in front of a creepy house, underneath a rising moon, with a murder of crows watching him.

He would go back along the driveway. He would follow the path and climb the wire fence and get his bike and go home. He would not be a part of this—whatever this was.

His chest was tight and his breath wheezy. When he reached into his backpack for his inhaler, though, he felt the slip of paper. His fingers curled around it, the note, about the club.

Lucas Hernandez had slipped it into his book, hadn't he? Which meant he would be there, didn't it? Maybe it was Lucas he'd seen in the upstairs window.

Find your way in.

Josh turned back to the house. Of course the front door

wouldn't work—that would be too easy. Clubs all had initiations, didn't they? Well, not his backgammon club. But other clubs—with more than one member—they always had something like this. It would all be okay, as soon as he got inside the house. And there was probably a way—a window or a door—on the side, or in the back. All he needed to do was be brave. If he was just brave enough, he would pass the test and be an official member of the Gorilla Club. Because the note had been real. From this world.

These were all the things going through his mind as he fought his way through bushes and brambles that grew next to the side of the house.

And then—the hole.

There's a funny thing about falling into a hole. Often, a person doesn't know they are falling until they've landed at the bottom. Josh thought that might be a poster quote, except the opposite of the inspirational kind.

When he was falling into the hole, he was shouting. And not in a brave way. He heard his voice from outside himself.

"Ahhhh!" he shouted. And then he landed.

The hole was deep and wide. Josh stayed in a crumpled ball and felt around for damage. His ankle was tender and his wrist was scratched, but they both still moved the way they were supposed to. The crow screeched from the side of the roof, right above him, and he thought, *Well, I still have my hearing.*

Because: Always Look on the Bright Side of Life.

He patted the ground around him, pushing away weeds and tall grasses, and discovered that the hole was rectangular in shape. Underneath the dirt and moss and weeds was cement. Everything made sense when Josh realized he'd fallen into a basement window well, the kind old houses often had. There had been one at his grandmother's house, back in Chicago. He and Big Brother used to play in it all the time.

The hole was not so deep that he couldn't easily climb out. But before he did that, he examined the space one more time. He pulled away a thick layer of climbing ivy and discovered the window.

Josh thought of the note. Had he found a way in?

He wiped off the grime and pressed his face close to the glass. It was dark, but he could make out the shadowy shapes of boxes and paint cans and a few scattered tools.

Opening a basement window of a stranger's house was against the law. He knew that. And there were NO TRESPASSING signs posted all over the place. Would Josh have broken the law if it hadn't been for the twig snapping? Or the footsteps?

Because that's what he heard right after the twig. Footsteps.

And the part of his mind that reacted to these sounds was not the law-abiding, rational part. It was the instinctual part. Fight or flight.

Josh knew he couldn't fight, and his best chance for flight was right in front of him. He turned back to the window, worked his fingers into the small crack, and pulled.

WHEN A DOOR IS SHUT

Another inspirational quote from Josh's dad: "When a door is shut, a window will open." It looked good on shiny poster paper, but like so many things, didn't actually translate to the real world.

The window didn't budge.

Josh stopped to listen. The footsteps had stopped, too. Josh's breath was loud and wheezy but he didn't want to take the time to open his backpack and get his inhaler. He was partly hidden there, in his hole. When the footsteps started again, Josh readjusted his grip. Splinters dug into his palms and his arms were shaking, but it didn't matter because Josh was pulling, lifting, yanking, with all the strength he had. Somehow it worked. The window opened, just wide enough for him to slide through.

He twisted around. Feet first, he began to lower himself.

Halfway through, he was stuck. His backpack—he'd forgotten to take it off and now he was wedged in the window, feet dangling.

The forest had gone quiet. Eerily quiet. And then another twig snapped and the footsteps started again.

Josh worked his arms out of the backpack straps. Then he inched his body the rest of the way through the window. Chest, shoulders, head. His fingers clung to the edge for a long time. He had no idea how far down the ground was. It was a terrible feeling, hanging on in the dark like that. His fingers slipped slowly, until they couldn't hang on any longer. Josh tumbled onto the cold concrete floor.

BASEMENT

Josh couldn't breathe. He'd been wheezing before, but the short drop to hard cement had knocked all the air out of him. And also, part of his body was missing.

No, wait. It was just his backpack that was missing.

His head cleared then, and his panic subsided, at least a little. Josh rolled to his knees and made his way back to the wall, judging the distance to the window. It was high but if he jumped, he could probably reach the dangling strap of his backpack.

He tried, but the pain in his ankle kept him low to the ground. He would have to go outside and around the house to get it.

Moving slowly and quietly, he felt his way through the dark, searching for stairs. He stumbled over something that clattered like metal as it slid across the floor. Josh froze, listening for a sound from the open window. And he heard it. It was the most ordinary sound in the world, but at that moment nothing could have scared him more.

Zzzzip.

Someone was on the other side of the window, opening his backpack.

Josh dropped to his hands and knees. He crawled to the darkest part of the basement. When his hand landed in a wet and slimy puddle, he got shakily to his feet and continued on, until his foot jammed against something hard. He reached down and gingerly felt around. It was a step.

If he just got up the stairs, he would be in the house. He would find the front door. He would get his backpack. Josh felt for the next step, and then the next. Slowly, tentatively, he began to climb.

THE BOX

Lucas found a backpack in the window well. It was the window well he and Maxie used to play in all the time. The rectangular hole was perfect for pretending they were in a ship, sailing to sea. Although sometimes they were in a rocket, blasting to Mars. And sometimes they were just in a hole, because that was fun, too.

When those memories filled up the space, Lucas tried his best to push them away and focus on the task at hand. He was there for a reason—to get Josh Duncan and take him home. Did the backpack mean he'd gone through the basement window? Lucas didn't want to think that, but the window was open and the kid wasn't around. He thought about calling out, but he didn't know if that would scare him.

He was still holding the shoebox he'd pulled from the darkest corner of his closet. He set it down to unzip the backpack.

If the backpack belonged to Josh Duncan, he'd have to go in after him. The clatter of metal from inside the basement made Lucas jump. Please don't be Josh Duncan, he whispered as he reached for the zipper. Please.

Zzzzip. The sound was loud in his ears. Hands trembling, Lucas reached into the backpack and pulled out a notebook. Even through the deepening dusk the moon was bright enough for him to see the cover. It said, *Josh Duncan, Mr. K's class.* Something else came out, too. The note he'd written and slipped into Josh Duncan's book of poetry.

Lucas leaned down to the open window. He was going to tell the kid to come back out—they'd go home together. That this whole thing was a bad mistake. But as he set the backpack down, he knocked the box on its side, scattering the objects that had been hidden away for years.

Lucas panicked. He bent close to the ground to gather them up. It was dark and damp in the hole, with so many weeds. His hands patted every inch of the space. He had to find them—every single one. Nothing else mattered. Even the sounds from the basement—the clatter of metal and the shuffling of feet. But when he heard the slam of the door, Lucas froze.

Josh Duncan had found the stairs. Josh Duncan was in the house.

STUPID PEOPLE IN
SCARY MOVIES

Josh hadn't meant to slam the basement door. But the door seemed to move on its own. Maybe it was because of old, brittle wood or the way the wind howled through the cracks in the boarded-up windows that made the door shut with such force, rattling the walls.

He should not have come—he knew that. He'd broken into an abandoned house in the middle of the forest, ignored a NO TRESPASSING sign and a barbed-wire fence. He'd lied to his mom. Everything was wrong.

Find your way in.

What did that even mean? And the Gorilla Club—was it even real? Why would he ignore his mom when she told him to floss his teeth, but would follow the directions of a crazy note written by a kid he didn't know?

These were the questions racing through his mind as he

tiptoed around the house, from the basement landing to the old kitchen and through to the dining room. The moon, spilling light between cracks, played tricks with his eyes. A room would be empty, and then with a blink, it appeared completely furnished with couches and chairs and tables. In the hallway, pictures appeared on the wall—family portraits and snapshots and school photos, just like Josh's mom was hanging back home. But when the light shifted, they were gone. It was like ghost furniture, flickering in and out between one world and another.

And there were sounds. At first he heard them coming from the basement. Footsteps on the wooden stairs. But then he heard something else. As Josh stood in the dining room, one sound grew louder. It seemed to be coming from the walls around him. Like something, or someone, was living inside the walls of the house. Someone who was crying.

Josh moved through the large front room. A door led to a foyer, with a stairway going to the second floor. He remembered the face he'd seen in the upstairs window. "Hello?" he whispered. He tried again, a little louder. "Hello?"

He still wanted to believe the meet-up was real. That Lucas had put the note in his book of poetry because there really was a Gorilla Club, and he was invited to be a new member. And maybe all the kids were upstairs, waiting for him. They were the ones doing the funny wailing noises or whatever. But what about the footsteps he'd heard outside? He couldn't stop thinking about the NO TRESPASSING sign. The barbed wire. Loser touches the house.

Josh turned to the front door. He put his hand on the knob. Yes, there'd been a note. And a face in the window. But there had also been footsteps and all the other things that made him know this was wrong. He'd wanted it so badly that he'd ignored all the danger signs, the warning signs. This whole thing was either a bunch of kids playing a mean joke on the new kid or—he didn't want to think about *or*.

A door slammed again, shaking the walls of the house. Josh knew it was the basement door. Whoever had been following him outside was now in the house. It didn't matter about the Gorilla Club or kids upstairs waiting or anything else. Josh needed to get home. He knew it, in his gut. He'd known it every step of the way but only then, when the footsteps were shuffling closer, did he hear what his gut had been trying to tell him.

To clarify: These thoughts took no time at all. He wasn't standing there like stupid people in scary movies, the ones who hesitate a second too long and then are doomed. No, Josh's thoughts at the moment weren't even thoughts, really. More like flashes of understanding, about his life and how he wanted to live it.

He grabbed the doorknob, twisted, and pulled. The door didn't budge.

The footsteps in the house were louder. Closer.

Josh pulled again. The front door was stuck. No, it wasn't stuck. It came back to Josh then, about the front door. He'd seen it from the outside—the sagging porch with its broken chair and boarded-up windows and, yes, boarded-up door. Josh was trapped.

Like a stupid person in a scary movie, he shot up the stairs.

SPILLED MILK

As Josh stumbled up the stairs, the howling of the wind through the cracks of the old house grew louder. There were other sounds, too, groans and creaks. Something with claws crept along the roof, directly above him.

All he could do was cling to the hope that there would be a Gorilla Club waiting for him upstairs. To calm himself, he recited the four short lines of the note, over and over. Gorilla Club. Saturday at Sundown. Follow the Map. Find Your Way In.

At the top of the stairs was a landing with a small window. The window let in just enough moonlight for Josh to make out a hallway, long and wide, with doors on either side. He thought back to the face he'd seen from the yard. That face—that person—had been in one of these rooms.

Josh put his hand on the first doorknob. He twisted and

pulled, but it wouldn't budge. When his breath came out with a wheeze, he remembered that his inhaler was in his backpack. Outside. He also remembered the quiet sound of the zipper and the slam of the basement door. Josh held his breath to listen. Was that a footstep? On the stairs?

Heart pounding, he moved to the second door. The moment his hand touched the knob he almost cried out. It was cold. So cold it seemed to burn his hand. And then—creak. There it was again. This time there was no mistaking the sound. It was a footstep, on the stairs. And then another. And another.

Josh moved to the third door. He reached out slowly, afraid to touch the knob. But the knob was warm and it turned easily. "Hello?" he whispered. The door swung open. Josh stepped inside.

It was cold, freezing cold inside the room. The full round moon shone in through the large open window. Shards of glass glittered across the floor.

Josh turned around slowly. "Hello?" A creak of a closet door seemed to answer him. The closet was in the far corner. The door was open.

Could this be it? The club thing? Because it didn't feel right. Not at all. He stood there waiting for something to happen, something normal, and in that waiting he heard them: footsteps, soft and steady, at the top of the stairs.

Josh crunched across broken glass to the closet and slipped inside. He closed the door behind him, but not all the way. He wanted to be able to hear what was happening with the footsteps, and he didn't want to shut out the sliver of moonlight. He leaned forward to listen. The footsteps were louder now. They were in the hallway. Josh crouched low and looked to the back of the closet. He would hide back there, as well as he could, until the footsteps went away.

The closet smelled terrible. Like dust and mold and old paint. Something else, too, that made his eyes sting. It was dark, and the farther he got from the narrow band of moonlight the darker it got. Still, Josh crawled to the very back, feeling his way around metal cans and crumpled newspapers and what felt like crusty old rags.

His hand brushed against something small and hard. He heard it slide across the floor and hit the wall on the other side of the closet. He patted around the floor until he located it, and rolled it around in his hand. It felt like a lighter, like the ones he'd seen at The Last Stop, next to the bundles of wood and worm sign.

He held it tightly and, for a moment, felt reassured. Yes, this whole thing had snowballed—or meat-loafed—out of control. There was no one here, which meant no Gorilla Club. It was just a joke.

And what about the face in the window? Had he really

seen it or had he just wanted to see someone up there, waiting for him. Or had it been one of *them*? Someone like Great-Aunt Evelyn or the pirate ship captain? He wished Big Brother would appear, to tell him what to do. Or at least tell him it would be okay. What would his dad say? Probably: There's No Use Crying over Spilled Milk.

Josh pressed himself into the corner, as far back as he could get. He listened for more footsteps. As soon as it was clear, he would go back to the basement. He would find a way to climb out. He would retrieve his backpack—he shook his head to get rid of the sound of the zipper. Why had someone opened it? Things were spinning out of control. Josh took a breath. "Three, six, nine, twelve . . . " When he got to ninety-nine, he began whispering the states in backward alphabetical order. "Wyoming, Wisconsin, West Virginia, Washington . . . "

At least the terrible creaking and wailing had stopped. He still heard clawed scurrying above his head, maybe coming from the attic. He looked to the open door that let in some of the moonlight. He held onto the lighter. Things were okay. They were going to be okay. He would not cry over spilled milk.

And then he saw them. In the other corner, right across from him. Two green eyes that glittered in the dark.

PUZZLE

The eyes blinked. A voice whispered. The whispers came together like words. The words came together but not in a normal way. More like a puzzle. When Josh finally pieced them together, he heard, "You made it. You found me. Welcome to the Gorilla Club."

He saw a sparkly rainbow.

All the others, the ones who had slipped through, had been predictable. Even the pirate ship captain. There had never been wailing walls or mysterious houses at dusk. Something was not right. Something was really wrong. And the smell—it was overpowering. He started to wheeze.

"What are you—what is this—" He wanted to know everything but didn't know what to ask.

"Paint thinner," she said, as if thinking he was asking about the smell. "And paint, turpentine, varnish stripper, polyurethane. From the last time the house was fixed up so it could be rented to nice people." And she laughed. The laugh seemed to make the walls tremble.

"What is going on?" Josh whispered. "What is happening?"

"It's a meeting. At my house. Our last member should be here soon." And just as she said it, a hulking figure filled the doorway, blocking out the moonlight.

THE CLOSET

When Lucas climbed the stairs and heard the walls softly wailing, his first thought was that it was coming from him. That's how deep his sadness was. And his fear. Maxie Moon had gone through a lot to get him into the house again. He shuddered to think why.

If not for the kid, the oddball kid in the ripped red raincoat, Lucas never would have come this far. And with each step, he told himself he was ready to turn back. But he couldn't. He couldn't let something bad happen again. That's what he was afraid of. Plus, he was responsible. He'd written the note, after all.

As much as he wanted to find Josh Duncan and get him out of the house, Lucas had no idea what he would say—about the note, or the house, or anything. The rock from his front porch was still in his pocket, and the old shoebox was clutched to his chest. He was carrying Josh's backpack, too.

He stood in the upstairs hallway, trying not to remember how it looked before the accident. How full of life and laughter the house had been. He wanted to be in his own home, with his parents and sisters. He wanted to be there more than anything. And he wanted to be done with the secret he'd been holding for too long.

Lucas moved slowly down the hallway, opening doors. When each room turned up empty, he stopped in front of the one in the middle, the one he knew it would be. It was the room he had spent so many happy hours as a little kid. He dreaded going inside.

The moon filled the room in such a peaceful and glowing way that it almost looked beautiful. Lucas stepped across broken glass to stand in front of the window. It was too much. He closed his eyes so he wouldn't have to see. And then he opened them. There was no going back. He turned to the closet.

Over the years he'd seen this closet door many times in his nightmares. But he wasn't prepared for how it would look in real life. He set down the shoebox and the backpack. He stepped toward the open door.

At first, he didn't see anything. So he stepped inside. The kid wasn't there, but he saw her. Or rather, he saw the eyes.

"Where is he?" he whispered.

No answer.

"I did what you asked. He's somewhere in the house. I

found his backpack outside the basement window." Lucas couldn't stop talking. It was like he was on trial, fighting to justify his—his what? Innocence? No.

His reason for being free of her? Maybe.

Why wasn't she speaking? Why were her eyes just staring like that, all green and glittering. He stepped closer, making sure that the door stayed open behind him. "I just want to help him get home," he whispered. "Please. Where is he?"

"I'm right here," a voice said softly. "Who are you talking to?"

Two things happened then: Lucas yelled, and the closet door slammed shut. Maybe it was from the wind, or maybe something else, but the door was supposed to stay open. All the time. Never close the door. Lucas was shouting, words that made sense and words that didn't. And he was twisting the doorknob. Twisting and pulling.

"It's okay," the soft voice said again. "I'm here. Nobody else is here."

Lucas turned around and pressed his back into the jammed door. A small flame of light appeared in the corner.

"Hold the lighter closer to your face," Maxie said. "So he can really see you."

Joshua Duncan followed her orders. And that's when Lucas fainted.

EARTHQUAKE

When the whole world shook like that, Josh was certain it was the big one. What was he supposed to do in an earthquake? Stop, drop, and roll? Stand in the doorway? Dive underneath a desk? He couldn't remember, so he yelled, "Earthquake!" and hoped someone would tell him what to do.

The girl said, "It's not an earthquake."

Josh opened his eyes. He hadn't known they were shut.

"It's Lucas," she continued. "He fainted."

Josh flicked the lighter and moved it closer to the lump of boy on the floor. Should he attempt CPR? He spun the lighter back to the girl. "What should we do?"

She didn't answer.

"Let's get him out of here."

"We can't," she said. "The door is stuck."

"How do you know?"

"See for yourself."

Josh inched his way to the door, reached up, and found the knob. He twisted and turned but it didn't budge. He scooted back to the kid, who was making mumbling sounds. "Wake up!" Josh said. "Hey!"

"Tell him a story," the girl said. "Tell him a ghost story."

Lucas was moving his head from side to side.

"He's waking—"

But before Josh could finish, Lucas was up. He grabbed Josh by the wrist, sending the lighter bouncing to the floor. Josh heard it slide and hit the wall. The small space was once again completely dark.

"What did you say?" Lucas demanded.

"What?"

"Who were you talking to just now?"

Josh Duncan had never been the brave one in any situation, but he found something new in himself at that moment. "What's wrong with you?" he asked.

"Just answer the question."

Josh sat in the dark with the question. He knew he'd been talking to the sparkly girl, the same way he'd always talked to his friends who were not part of the real world. He knew the girl had first told him about the Gorilla Club.

"Did you put the note in my book?"

"Please, just answer my question. Who were you talking to?"

There was something Josh was missing. A piece of the puzzle he was not seeing. What had happened right before Lucas fainted? The answer dawned on him, in a moment that was impossible to describe.

"You see her?" Josh whispered. "You see her, too?"

When he said it, the earth seemed to shake again.

Josh dropped down and felt around for the lighter. He thought about Big Brother and Great-Aunt Evelyn and the parade of people who had populated his young life. He hadn't ever considered that someone else might be able to see them, too.

The world started to spin. Josh was on a dark and spinning ride where one more word, from either of them, would send him flying somewhere he didn't want to go. He was cold and hot at the same time. He found the lighter and flicked it on. Then he clutched his stomach and understood why Lucas had fainted. The world didn't make sense anymore.

"I think I'm going to be sick."

Lucas lunged and grabbed the lighter from Josh's hand. He held it up to his face, right into his eyes. Josh blinked, then wrapped his arms around Lucas's waist and tried to wrestle him to the ground. "Give me back the lighter!"

"What are you doing? Are you crazy?"

"Give me the lighter!"

The boys took turns kicking and swinging. Josh crashed into the back of the closet, scattering a pile of cans. He felt something wet seep into his pants and he jumped up fast. "What is it? What is it?"

A new chemical smell filled the closet. Lucas and Josh were locked in some sort of cartoon wrestling match. Neither one had fought in their lives, but now they were punching wildly into the air. Lucas took a swing and slipped on the wet floor. He landed on his back and shrieked. "What is this? Did you puke?"

"No, I didn't puke!" Josh didn't think he puked. That's how odd everything was. Maybe he did puke?

"Then what did I just roll in?"

Josh remembered the list she'd recited. "Turpentine and varnish stripper and some other stuff. I don't know. It's the stuff people use to fix up a house. She told me that. For the next people."

The fumes in the closet made them both feel sick. Josh had the lighter in his hand. He flicked it on. "I think there are rags back there," he said. "To clean it up." He picked up a hardened rag and started wiping up the mess. The air suddenly seemed different.

"Move it around," Lucas said. "The lighter."

Hands trembling, Josh held it high. He moved it slowly around the small space.

"She's gone," Lucas said flatly. "Now we're stuck."

Josh felt his chest getting tight. The smell in the closet was making it worse. He reached for his backpack, to get his inhaler, and then remembered. "You didn't happen to bring my backpack, did you? When you followed me and trapped me in here?"

"I brought it up," Lucas said. "But it's out there. On the other side of the door. And don't say it that way, okay? I didn't want to trap you. I came to make sure you were okay."

"But the note—"

"Yeah, I'm sorry about that."

Josh held the lighter closer to Lucas. Silence filled the closet as they stood in the dark with one tiny flame between them. Then, at the exact same time, the two boys lunged for the door. They pounded until their knuckles were bruised.

SECRET PASSAGE

Lucas remembered the stone in his pocket. He wrapped his fingers around it and, for some reason, felt a moment of peace. He could hear Josh Duncan behind him, knocking at the back wall of the closet. "What are you doing?" he asked.

"Looking for a secret passage."

Lucas didn't tell him it was hopeless. He'd spent hours in this very closet as a young kid, and he knew every inch of it. There was no secret passage.

Josh stopped knocking. His breath was shallow and wheezy. He crawled next to Lucas and the two sat in the dark without speaking. It might have only been three minutes of silence, but three minutes in the dark can be a long time. Like three minutes of making a speech can be long. Three minutes of eating in the cafeteria can be long. Three minutes of standing in your underwear in the locker room can be long.

Josh closed his eyes and tried to take deep breaths. The dark was different behind his closed eyes, more familiar and comfortable, like going home. Who knew? Who knew the dark behind a person's own eyelids could feel so safe compared with the dark all around? He sat up straight and opened his eyes. It was just as dark. He flicked on the lighter. "Does anyone know you're here?"

"No," Lucas said. "You?"

"No. Why did you give me the note? About the club? I thought it was real."

"She told me what to write. She said she'd go away if I did it. And then I felt bad. And I got worried for you. So I came here, to make sure you'd be okay. And now—"

Josh wheezed. "Now neither one of us is okay."

Lucas said, "You're not going to die, are you?"

"I could use my inhaler. And a secret passage."

"Please don't die. I couldn't take another ghost in my life."

"Keep talking," Josh said. "It helps."

Which is how Lucas Hernandez told his story. The one he'd been hiding his whole life. The one that haunted him. He told his ghost story in the dark. The way all ghost stories should be told.

GHOST STORY

"We moved here when I was five," Lucas said. "Right before I started kindergarten."

"Kleenex," Josh blurted.

"What?"

"Nothing, sorry. Keep going."

Lucas cleared his throat. "I've never told anyone this before, so don't go shouting things out unless there's a reason."

"It was a thing that happened in kindergarten," Josh tried to explain. "I got teased a lot."

"Oh. Sorry."

"That's okay. Keep going. I think it's helping." His breath sounded less shallow.

Lucas continued. "I was sort of shy, I guess. I played a lot of things by myself."

"I was like that, too," Josh said.

"So at school, I remember going out to the playground and this girl came over and took my hand. She just took my hand and it didn't seem weird. She said, 'I'll be your best friend if you'll be mine.' And I said I would—be her best friend. I liked her right away because she wore two different-colored shoes. And she liked sparkly clothes. We were together every second after that first time on the playground, every second we could be. At her house or my house. We liked to look for rocks." His voice trailed off and all the freakiness was gone for a moment, replaced by a plain old sadness.

Josh said, "So, wait—she was real? I mean—"

"Yes. What did you think?"

"She wasn't like she is now?"

"What? Of course not. She was my friend."

"Okay," Josh said, beginning to understand. "What happened?"

Lucas took a deep breath. When he started talking again, his voice was different. "When she died, I guess I just didn't believe it. When my parents told me what happened, I was six, in first grade. But I kept seeing her everywhere, so I didn't understand why everyone else was so sad. I saw her in class still, and on the playground. At the grocery store. Everywhere. I made my mom take me to her gravesite. I guess I tried to dig it up, to prove she wasn't in there. I don't really remember, but that's what they told me. Crazy, huh?"

"Not crazy," Josh said.

"But then I sort of stopped seeing her. I made some new friends. And I guess I just forgot about it. Things were normal for a little while."

Josh was thinking about his old backyard. The hole he dug in the dirt. The rock with Big Brother's name carefully painted.

"But then, on the first day of school this year, she showed up again. She didn't look the same. I mean, it was like she was in fifth grade, too. She grew up." He paused. "When we were in kindergarten she would stand on the little kid side and stare at the big kids. She'd say 'We get to be over there, Lucas. When we're in fifth grade.' I'd forgotten that until now."

Josh cleared his throat. He wanted to tell Lucas about Big Brother, but Lucas kept talking.

"I didn't recognize her, not at first. I actually thought she was a real kid, a new kid. But then she said things, about when we were little. And about what happened. And then she started looking weird and following me and sitting on the edge of my desk and cheering when I was playing soccer or running around the track. I didn't know what to do. And then she wanted to talk about the thing that happened. The day she died. And—and—I knew that if she did, I wouldn't be able to take it—" His voice broke. He started to cry.

"Hey—" Josh scooted over and placed his hand on Lucas Hernandez's shoulder.

Lucas sniffed. "There's more."

It was like a nightmare, Josh thought. And we're both trapped in it. The only way out was to go all the way to the end. But what if it was the kind of nightmare that getting to the end was the thing that killed you?

"I thought I'd just ignore her and maybe she'd go away. So when she followed me to class, I pretended I didn't see her. And when she told me jokes in the lunch line, I ignored her." Lucas paused. "Knock-knock."

"What?"

"Knock-knock."

"Who's there?"

"Europe."

"Europe who?"

"No I'm not."

"I don't get it," Josh said.

"It sounds like poo—you're a poo."

"That's not even funny."

"I know."

"So what happened next?"

"You showed up. That's what happened next. And for some reason, she was interested in you. I thought it was just because you were new. That's what I thought. I thought it was because you didn't know about this house, like everyone else did. So she saw you as someone she could get to come here.

And that's why she had me write the note. I think it was her way to get me to come." He paused. "How's your breathing?"

"Better," Josh said. "But why did she want you to come here?"

Lucas lowered his voice again. "I have these dreams—"

"What? I can't hear you."

"I have these dreams. Where she's in this closet. Only this time I know it. I open the door for her. I save her."

"So when she died—" Josh was getting nervous. He flicked on the lighter and held it close to Lucas's face.

"We used to play in here all the time. Maxie's nonna had a lighter we liked because it looked like a ship. We weren't supposed to play with it, but sometimes Maxie would sneak it in. We knew we would never actually use it, you know— light it. We just liked how it looked. But on that day, the day it happened, I had to go home and she wasn't done playing. She told me to close the door. She didn't want Nonna to find her with the lighter. And that was the other thing—we weren't supposed to close the door all the way. Ever. I don't think I closed it when I left, but I must have. Because it was stuck. That's what happened. She used the lighter. And the door was stuck."

Josh flicked off the flame.

THE THING
THAT SETS HARRY
HOUDINI FREE

When he could speak again, Josh said, "We need to get out of here."

"I know that. Of course I know that."

"Then why did you shut the door?"

"I didn't shut it. The wind must have. Or she did."

Josh felt his neck start to twitch. He thought of his mom at home, hanging pictures. "Why? Why does she want us here? Why doesn't anyone live here?" He remembered the little kids at the obstacle course. The house in the woods. *Loser touches the house.*

"After the accident her family moved. The fire didn't burn for long, but the smoke. The smoke—the smoke is what—" He choked on the words, couldn't get the last ones out. Then he said, "They tried to rent it out. Families move in but there are noises. Doors slam and people hear, they hear a girl crying in the walls. Most of them don't last a year." Lucas was done talking. He was done except for a whisper, "I don't think we'll ever get out of this closet. I don't think she will let us."

Josh tried to make sense of the story he'd heard. "Why did she do this? Why did she bring us both here?"

"She wants us to die."

"No. That's not it. I don't know her reason, but maybe figuring it out is the key." His own words made Josh remember a quote from his Harry Houdini book, the one from the haunted library.

"Listen," he said. "My brain is the key that sets me free. Harry Houdini said that."

Lucas sniffled. "I thought he swallowed pins to get out of stuff."

"Yeah, but you know what I mean."

"Hey." Lucas's voice brightened. "You just made me think of something. There's this thing on YouTube. *Real Life Stunts*. Have you seen it?"

"No," Josh said.

"It's basically how to do all the things you see in movies, but for real. Like break down a door with your foot, for example."

"And you just thought of that now?"

"Do you want to try it or not?"

"Yes," Josh said. "Definitely."

The two boys scrambled to their feet, knocking against each other in the small space. Josh held up the lighter and flicked it on.

"I'll count to three," Lucas said. "We need to aim for the space right next to the doorknob. On the videos it works every time. Aim for that spot."

Josh moved the lighter. "There?"

"Exactly."

Lucas put his arm around Josh for balance. Josh turned off the lighter and slipped it in his pocket, then shifted to one foot and held on to Lucas.

Lucas started the countdown. "One," he said. The boys clutched tighter.

"Two—" They shifted their weight and lifted their legs.

"Three!" The two boys kicked with all their might. There was a tremendous noise, but nothing more.

"I think I cracked my leg bone," Josh said.

"Yeah," Lucas agreed. "Me too. Should we try it again?"

Josh lifted his leg and shook it around. He figured the fact that it could move meant it probably wasn't really broken. "Can we switch sides?"

"Good idea."

Clumsily the boys shuffled around each other. Josh flicked on the lighter again, to help find the right spot on the door.

"Keep it on," Lucas said. "It helps if we can see the door."

Josh set the lighter close to their feet. He wanted to believe that the tiny bit of light would help. He wanted to believe that they could kick the door down, just the way Lucas had described. My brain is the key that sets me free, he reminded himself.

He felt like he'd been sucked into an alien ship or shoved off a cliff holding a ten-pound bowling ball. Because the truth was, they were trapped in the closet because a dead girl wanted them there. She had orchestrated the whole thing. It was hard to believe that a couple of well-placed kicks would do anything to thwart her plan, whatever it was. Which meant that she controlled what happened next. Not Josh, not Lucas, not a YouTube channel about busting down doors.

The more Josh thought about it, the more his chest squeezed tight. So he clung to his new friend and visualized the most amazing kick—a kick that would set them free.

And it was funny because, right then, Lucas Hernandez did feel like a friend. Like maybe one hour of locked-in-a-closet time equaled an entire year in the real world. Josh briefly wondered whether it was the kind of thing that would last outside the closet or whether his life would go back to how it was before, when he ate his lunch on Dead Melanie's bench. Then he wondered whether they would get out at all.

"You ready?" Lucas asked him. "On three?"

"On three," Josh said, like an official door buster. A part of a door-busting team. It was the first time he'd felt something close to being on a team. Even though it didn't come under the best of circumstances, it was a good feeling.

Lucas counted and they kicked. They kicked hard. The world exploded in fireworks behind Josh's eyes—that's how hard he kicked. The door seemed to buckle for a moment. Then there was a laugh. A girl's laugh.

"Did you hear that?" Josh opened his eyes. The door was still there. "Did you hear the laugh? Why is she laughing? Is this a game? Is she still thinking like a little kid? Tell me more about her. There's a reason she wanted us here."

Lucas didn't answer. His shoulders shook. He sank down in front of the door. "I can't believe this is happening."

Josh crouched low and looked him in the face. He could see that Lucas had given up. "Lucas, we can do this. Let's try again."

Lucas shook his head. Josh glanced past him to the lighter at their feet. It took him a moment to register the small fire creeping along the trail of spilled liquid. Tiny sparks were catching on the twisted rags and old newspapers they'd used as mops.

Lucas saw the fire, too. Both boys froze as the flames grew quickly, lapping up the chemicals and spewing out a thick cloud of smoke.

Josh had prepared himself for earthquakes and volcanoes and Bigfoot and bear attacks. He knew not to talk to strangers. He carried his inhaler everywhere. He wore a bike helmet. He didn't cross a street without looking both ways. And he never ever *ever* played with matches. So how did this happen?

He kicked at the door. He beat it with his fist. The smoke stung his eyes. He fought to take in good air. He didn't even notice Lucas shouting, "Josh, give me your coat!"

Because a thought was forming. It was coming together like a quiet voice in all the commotion. "It's the second meeting of the Gorilla Club, Josh," the voice said. "What do you see?"

And as Lucas was ripping the coat off his back, Josh looked around. What was he missing? What was he not seeing?

He looked at every wall and corner. He looked at the door again and its hinges.

Then he did the one thing he hadn't thought to do. He looked up.

WHEN YOU
ARE TRAPPED
IN A CLOSET

"I knew there must be a reason you wore that thing every-where," Lucas said, trying to make a joke as he beat the rest of the dying flames with Josh's new red raincoat. But the joke couldn't cut through the thick, gray, choking smoke that was now trapped in the closet with them.

Josh pointed to the ceiling and the attic door he'd glimpsed when the flames were strong. When Lucas didn't see, because of the smoke, Josh grabbed him by the arm. "There's a door in the ceiling," he said. "In the back corner. If you lift me up—"

Lucas didn't wait for him to finish. He placed himself in the back corner. "Here?"

"I think so," Josh said.

When Lucas crouched over, Josh climbed onto his back. Josh could feel him shake as he struggled to straighten.

"Can you reach?"

Josh stretched for the ceiling but his fingers barely skimmed. "Higher," he called. And to himself he whispered, "Please. Please let this work." He forced one foot onto Lucas's shoulder and then the other. He wobbled there, fighting for balance. Then slowly, steadily, he straightened his legs. He reached up. He felt around until he could trace the frame of the attic door. "Please," he whispered again. "Please open." He placed his hands flat in the center and he pushed. Tentatively at first, and then so hard his arms shook.

He heard a creak of wood before he felt the movement. Just an inch, but a shower of attic dust fell into his eyes.

"Hold on!" Lucas shouted, tightening his grip on Josh's trembling legs.

Josh squeezed his eyes shut and pushed at the door again. Again and again, until he felt another shift. "Get me higher!"

Lucas was on the verge of collapsing, but he said, "You can do it, Josh!" And he gave one more heave.

More than anything else, the words were exactly what Josh needed to hear. Not from Big Brother or his dad or a poster, but words from a real live kid who needed him.

This time, when Josh pushed at the attic door, it opened all the way. More dust and debris rained down on the boys, including chewed-up paper and fluff from nests made by generations of squirrels.

Along with their nests and dust, the squirrels dropped into

the closet. They fell on Josh's head, clawed at his hair, and then tumbled down his body. "Ahhhh!" he screamed.

"What is it? What is—" And then, "Ahhhh!" Lucas shouted. "Something is scratching me—what is it?"

Josh felt Lucas losing his grip. He stretched his arms into the hole. "I'm almost there—push me higher—"

"There are all these animals in here. They have claws!"

Josh could hear the panic in his voice, but he couldn't call back. He didn't have enough strength or breath. He thrust his head inside. A small attic window let the moonlight in and illuminated dozens of wild and startled eyes.

"AHHH!" Josh screamed when he saw them.

"AHHH!" Lucas screamed in response. "What is it? What's up there?"

Josh felt his head sinking. He reached up and anchored one arm on the attic floor. "Push me higher!"

Josh felt Lucas give one more push before his grip slipped away. Josh held on and inched his way up. He shimmied onto his stomach and then flipped around to reach his hand to Lucas.

When Lucas jumped to catch his hand and Josh tried to heave him up, it seemed they were about to experience the miraculous car-accident superpower moment Josh'd always heard about. But then Lucas just dangled there, not moving. It was so preposterous that the boys almost burst out laughing.

How was Josh supposed to pull him up? How did he think, even for a minute, that it would work?

Lucas dropped down. He fought another cough. "These things are squirrels. And they are crazy. You have to get me out of here."

The good news was the smoke was clearing from the closet, rising into the attic and floating out through the busted window. Josh felt so much relief, until he looked back down and saw what was happening.

The dry nesting material that had rained down into the closet was perfect tinder for a few leftover sparks. Another small flame grew quickly.

"Go around!" Lucas shouted, grabbing for Josh's coat. "There's a door in the corner of the attic floor. It looks like a trapdoor. Get out of the attic and come to the room. Maybe the door will open from the other side. Or maybe you can run for help."

"Lucas!"

Lucas was coughing again, and beating at the flames. "Hurry! I'll be okay. Just hurry!"

Josh got to his feet. His legs were shaking. His head bumped on the low part of the ceiling. The walls were wailing again, with sobs and cries for help.

"We'll get you out," Josh said to the crying walls. He was saying it to Lucas. He was saying it to himself.

He pushed through cobwebs and shadows to the far end of the attic. Just as Lucas had said, there was a door in the floor. Josh yanked on the handle and it opened easily. But whatever kind of steps had once been there were gone now. It was just a deep dark hole. Josh held on to the edge of the door and swung his legs down. He had no idea how far the drop was, and he was terrified, but he didn't hesitate. He let go, into the darkness. His legs buckled when he hit the ground and a sharp pain shot up the same ankle he'd hurt when he'd fallen in the window well. Josh stayed on the floor, clutching his ankle and gasping for breath until he remembered Lucas, trapped in a closet. Then he found his way to his feet, even with the shooting pain.

He stumbled down the same hallway as before, but nothing looked the same. The doors were all wide open and every room was furnished, like people still lived there. In the moonlight he saw it—the wallpaper and paintings and photos lining the walls.

Gasping, limping, he ran past it all, straight to the room in the very center with the shards of broken glass and the terrible closet door. He put his hand on the door lightly, like he'd seen from firefighter demonstrations, and was relieved it wasn't hot. "Lucas," he shouted. "I'm here!" Lucas pounded his response.

This was it. This was everything. There was a terrible

moment when Josh turned the knob and wondered if he would be able to open it. No, he would open it. He had to.

He pulled. The door flew open and Lucas Hernandez tumbled out. Three screeching balls of fur and claws scurried across the floor and to the open window. Black, billowing smoke filled the room and then floated away. The boys collapsed in the middle of the room, gulping in cold night air.

Josh grabbed his backpack. He pulled out his inhaler.

"Are you okay?" Lucas asked. He was clutching a shoebox to his chest.

Josh nodded. "You?"

"I don't know," Lucas said shakily. "I still don't understand what she wants. What she'll do next."

With those words, the boys scrambled to their feet. They made sure the fire was completely extinguished and there were no injured squirrels before helping each other to the hallway and then down the stairs. Getting out the basement window seemed easy after what they'd just been through.

When they were in front of the house, looking up at the broken window, Lucas said, "Your coat!"

Josh knew the coat was ruined. "It doesn't matter," he said. He remembered, before the move, his mom shopping for the biggest, most indestructible raincoat she could find. She'd wanted a coat to protect him from anything, and it did.

ANOTHER TOUCHDOWN

They were back where they started—at the NO TRESPASS-ING sign by the barbed-wire fence where two bicycles leaned against a tree. There was still so much to understand, but none of it seemed understandable.

They walked their bikes across the meadow to the dirt pile next to the skeleton house. Josh looked up at the stars. He couldn't stop thinking about the crying walls and the closet and the little girl who died in the fire. The attic and the squirrels and the ghost story told in the dark. He remembered the little kids, riding up and down that very mound of dirt—it seemed so long ago. "I can't go home yet," he said.

Lucas said, "Me neither."

It wasn't like they made a plan. They just started to ride. They rode on the smooth streets of Bear Creek housing development, peering into lighted windows. They saw families gathered at tables and in front of television sets. It made the world feel almost normal.

Still, when they got to the waving bear, they turned away from the houses. The same bright moon lit the way as they found themselves on the road back to school. They rode through the bus zone and the walkway. Left their bikes at the edge of the playfield and walked to the high school stadium.

When they reached the fence, Lucas said, "Let's go inside." He was still carrying the box.

As soon as Josh's feet touched the spongy black surface, he started to run. His ankle was sore but he sprinted across the springy lanes, right onto the football field. As he raced across the smooth green grass, he thought, This is it. This is why people run.

He heard Lucas behind him, shouting something.

"What?" Josh called.

"Go long!" Lucas shouted. "For the pass!"

It took Josh a moment to understand what he meant, and then he realized, I'm playing football! He looked up, over his shoulder, and a football appeared in the sky. It crossed the moon and soared above him in a magical, spiraling arc. Josh reached out his arms and made a giant leap. His body felt weightless, and the ball dropped perfectly into his outstretched hands.

Tucking it under his arm, just like the Panthers did on

Friday night, Josh dodged his way to the end zone. With Lucas on his heels, he dove for a touchdown and his shoulder hit the ground with a thud. He stayed on the ground with his face in the grass, closed his eyes and heard the crowd call his name. Then they stopped and the football disappeared because it was never there. But the grass—it still smelled amazing.

Josh lifted his head. "You should smell this grass."

Lucas sat next to him. He leaned over and sniffed. "It smells like grass," he said. Then he wiped his face with the back of his hand.

They'd been trapped together in a closet. They'd scratched and pounded and kicked at a door. It all came back to them, in that moment. Everything. Sitting in the end zone, smelling grass, they tried to fit it into normal life.

Josh lay on his back and looked up at the night sky. Lucas stretched out next to him. He said, "I keep waiting for her to show up."

"Why did she do it? The note? The closet?"

Lucas clutched the box even tighter and said, "I don't know."

The night air was damp and chilly but the two boys stayed like that, looking up at the stars. In that moment, the universe seemed so big and impossible to understand that Josh felt he couldn't understand it completely. He imagined all the other solar systems out there, all the different possibilities for life.

And then he thought, what if they weren't all out there? What if there were different universes all around them? And what if sometimes, just sometimes, the spaces between them were visible?

Lucas said, "You know how in all the ghost stories, the ghosts are always coming back for a reason? Like unfinished business or revenge or something?"

"I guess," Josh said, although he'd never really thought of it that way.

"I thought that was what she was doing to me. You know, punishing me."

"You didn't know she was going to get locked in the closet. Or use the lighter." Josh glanced over at Lucas, holding on to the box. He thought about the boxes in his own house, closed up and labeled. He thought about his mom and the family photos hanging on the wall. He missed Big Brother.

Something occurred to him then, lying underneath the big sky. He thought, What if it's not them that need to come back, but us needing them? What if that's what brings them back?

"I'm sorry about the note," Lucas said. "I didn't think you'd find it. And then, when I wasn't sure, I came after you. I'm sorry I scared you like that. I'm really sorry."

Josh was still pondering the ghost thing. "But that's just it. You did everything you could to help me. To protect me. Even

though you were scared. Don't you see? You went back to the place that scared you the most, and you saved me. I think—"
He stopped.

He wanted to say that Maxie Moon hadn't come back to hurt Lucas. But that Lucas had been the one keeping his pain alive, all along. It was a hard thing to put into words. So instead Josh said, "You would have saved her if you'd known." And when he heard Lucas let out a deep sigh, he knew he'd said the right thing.

"Marvelous Mystery!" Lucas Hernandez exclaimed suddenly.

"What?"

"Just—everything. Don't forget, okay?"

"How could I forget it?" But Josh knew what he meant.

When Lucas said, "I don't feel as bad anymore," the thought came to Josh again, that maybe ghost stories weren't about the ghosts as much as about the people who saw them.

He thought about sitting on Dead Melanie's bench, day after day. How no one looked over. How he had become invisible. How he couldn't even wear jeans because he was afraid they would make a noise. How it didn't seem right to stay quiet anymore, invisible anymore. Because he was in this world. He wasn't in the other one.

So he told Lucas all that. His voice sounded too loud and too weird in his own ears, but he kept talking anyway.

Josh waited until he didn't think Lucas was going to say anything. Then, after a moment, Lucas said, "There was this one time. I was waiting for my mom to pick me up from school, but she had to work late so my grandma came. My abuela. She stood outside the car and called for me. But she called me what she always called me at home—Pollito. Do you know what that means?"

Josh shook his head.

"It means little chicken. But in a good way. Except some of my friends heard her and thought it was funny. They started calling me Little Chicken. So I asked her not to call me that anymore. Even at home. And now she's gone. And all I can think about is how much I loved hearing her voice. I'd do anything to hear her call me Pollito again. And that's—that's what I'm thinking about Maxie right now, too."

Josh stood. He offered his hand. Lucas took it and Josh pulled him up, and the two boys stood in the middle of the field, feeling big and small at the same time.

SUNDAY

They didn't talk on the bike ride home. They were all talked out. They barely said goodbye when Josh turned in at the waving bear. So many thoughts were racing through his head. He tried to push them away, but they swirled and danced, almost teasing him with something he should know. He knew it was about Big Brother.

Josh braced himself before going into the house. He would have to explain his missing coat and the smell of smoke and how late it was and everything else. But when he walked into the living room, his mom was asleep on the couch, surrounded by boxes and photographs. He left her there, limped up the stairs, and climbed into bed.

Sunday morning was bright and sunny. That was one good thing, Josh thought. He wouldn't need to tell his mom about the raincoat. Not yet.

She'd been full of questions since he'd slumped down the stairs for breakfast. He tried to answer without giving anything away, and the whole exchange gave him a big headache. So he excused himself to do homework, and that's where he stayed most of the day. Big Brother didn't show up, even though Josh got out the Lego.

There was one thing Josh was most worried about, something he wished he'd asked Lucas on their ride home in the dark. He wished he'd asked what things would be like on Monday morning, when they saw each other in Mr. K's class. Would they be friends? Or would it be too weird? Would Josh still be too weird? He really wished he knew.

MARVELOUS MYSTERY

Mr. K clapped. "Ready-set?"

The class shouted, "You-bet!" They settled in their seats as Mr. K looked at the Marvelous Mystery sign-up sheet. "Mr. Hernandez—are you ready to wow us with your knowledge?"

Lucas stood. He picked up the large board with the perfect miniature replica of Stonehenge and also a plain brown shoebox. He walked to the front of the class and set the board and the box on the presentation table. He cleared his throat. The faces of his classmates were blurry.

Since the beginning of the school year, he'd been thinking about this project. It had opened his eyes to the mysteries all around him. He wondered if that's what Mr. K had in mind, back when he assigned it. He thought it was an amazing miracle that Mr. K showed the video with the gorilla, and that he and Josh Duncan had both seen it.

"Stonehenge is one of the most famous landmarks in Great Britain," he started. "And to make this replica of it, I went out and I found rocks. When I was looking for the perfect rocks, I wondered about the people who built Stonehenge. I wondered what they saw in the rocks they picked. And why they placed them in the circle the way they did. I bet they had no idea that all these thousands of years later, people would be looking at their rocks, and wondering so much about them."

He picked up the shoebox and lifted the lid. He took out rock after rock and set them on the table with care. "This is a collection I started back when I was five. With my best friend. We loved looking for rocks together. Some of you might remember her, but we never talk about her, do we? But I want to talk about her now. So that's what my presentation is today. I'm going to tell you about the marvelous mystery of Maxie Moon." Lucas didn't tell them about all the stuff that happened after she died. He didn't talk about the closet or the fire or her family moving away. He just talked about her, the sparkly girl who was his best friend. The girl who had always wanted to be in fifth grade, on the big kid side.

On Sunday, when he was getting ready for his presentation, Lucas examined each and every rock he and Maxie had collected together. His sisters said, "Why are you laughing about a rock?" And then a moment later, "Why are you crying about a rock?"

All he could say was, "It's a marvelous mystery."

It took being locked in a closet to see her again—really see. She hadn't wanted to hurt him. What happened with him and Josh and the closet and the fire was an accident. Lucas didn't blame her. And for the first time since her death, he didn't blame himself.

And what about the Gorilla Club? Why the meeting? In the house? He might not ever know all the reasons, but maybe it was as simple as this: Maxie Moon had found a new friend, and she'd wanted Lucas to find him, too.

As Lucas continued his Marvelous Mystery presentation, holding up rock after rock and describing his best friend who had found them with him, he searched the room for two faces, but he only saw one. So he smiled, right into the eyes of his new friend, Josh Duncan.

LAST MEETING

After school, Josh was on the floor in his room, surrounded by piles of Lego. He was ready to start building but couldn't pick up the first piece. He still hadn't seen Big Brother, and the Lego made him think of him even more. So when Big Brother suddenly appeared, Josh was flustered. He didn't know what to say.

Big Brother spoke first. "I'm sorry for all that. Being so bossy."

"No, it's my fault. And I'm glad you're back. I've missed you."

"I've missed you, too."

Josh said, "It's been completely crazy around here."

"I know."

"You do?"

"Sure. I'm never far away."

Josh picked up a base and a set of wheels. "You want to build?"

"Sure," Big Brother said. But he just sat back against the bed and watched. "When I first came back, we made a deal. Do you remember?"

Josh shrugged. Already he didn't like where this was going.

"I want you to think about something, Josh. Do you remember what was going through your mind that night in the house?"

Josh closed his eyes and saw it again. "What are you trying to say?"

"I think you know."

Josh opened his eyes. "You'd better get started if you don't want me to use up all the good pieces."

"I want you to tell me what happened."

Josh thought about how to say it. It had happened fast, in a flash of a moment, and it had been so big and so small at the exact same time.

"I was thinking about Mom and Dad," he started. "And all our invisible things. And it was like I finally knew they didn't have all the answers for me. That I had to come up with some on my own. That I *had* to. And later, I looked at the sky. It went on forever. And it was so full of things. Things I could see and things I couldn't. We think we know everything but we don't. Does that make any sense?"

"Yes."

"And you know what else?" Josh was amped up. All the thoughts that had been simmering in his mind were bubbling over.

"What?"

"Thinking about Mom and Dad like that, like they didn't know everything in the universe anymore? It was weird."

"It is weird," Big Brother said. "It's called growing up. And you know what?"

"What?"

"It was truly brave, what you did. And you probably don't need this from me, but I'm proud of you."

"I do need it," Josh said. "I always need it."

Big Brother shook his head. "Not anymore."

Josh knew he was trying to tell him something, something more than how proud he was. "You're going away, aren't you?"

When Big Brother didn't answer, Josh thought about Maxie Moon and Great-Aunt Evelyn and all the friends he used to have, including the pirate ship captain. He thought about the gorilla and how people can't always see what's right in front of them.

He tried again. "You can stay. Right? Stay just like this?"

"I don't think so, Little Bro."

Josh said, "The photograph. Of the baby. Is that why you came back?"

"What do you think?"

Josh shrugged. "I thought maybe you could tell me."

"Tell you what?"

"Tell me about you."

"I'm your big brother," he said, ruffling Josh's hair. "Tell me what you want me to say."

Josh changed the subject and asked him what kind of Lego world they should build this time. Big Brother said castle—it had always been his favorite. So Josh worked on the castle and didn't look at him. They sat like that for a long time, until the room got dark and the castle was nearly complete.

Then he said, "Well, Little Bro, I need to get going." And it felt different to Josh—different from all the other times he'd been ready to leave.

Josh said, "I don't want to grow up if it means I can't see you." He started to cry.

Big Brother moved in close and put his arm around Josh and the two just sat there until things didn't feel so sad. Josh wiped his face.

"You'll be okay," Big Brother said.

Josh took a deep breath. "Where are you going exactly?"

Big Brother shrugged. "You know that girl?"

Josh remembered the night of the football game. Two shadowy figures walking together across the field. "From the game?"

"Yeah. We've been hanging out. We're just going to take off for a while."

"Oh."

"Be good to Mom and Dad," he said.

"I will."

"Stay out of burning closets."

Josh laughed. "I will."

"Push at your own edges."

Josh laughed again, even though the tears were back again. He could tell Big Brother was almost gone. "Hey!" he called. "Big Brother—"

"Yeah?"

"The girl—the one you've been hanging out with. Does she have a name?"

"Of course she does, doofus."

"What is it? What's her name?" Even before he said it, Josh knew what the answer would be. He knew.

"Melanie," he said. "Melanie Price." And then he was gone.

Josh sat for a few minutes. His neck twitched once, and he waited for the next one but it didn't come.

"Go, Big Brother," he whispered. "The happiest years of your life." Then, when his legs stopped shaking enough to stand, he went downstairs to find his mother.

NOTHING
IS MISSING

She was sitting on the couch. Josh stood in front of her. "Mom—" He tried to sound normal. "Remember when you made me bury my imaginary big brother?"

"Yes," she said.

"Why did you do that? I mean, why was it such a big deal to you?"

"Kids at school were teasing you," she said. "It was interfering with your social skills and development—"

"I know all that. But I've been thinking. I had other imaginary friends. But Big Brother was the one that always bothered you."

"You were too old—"

"I know," he said. "But what was it really? Why did he bother you the most? What about the old captain? With the wooden leg? You weren't so worried about him."

She pulled her eyes away and stared at the photo on the wall, the one with the baby. "It just made me sad," she said finally, in the smallest voice Josh had ever heard coming from her. "You should have had a big brother. You *did* have a big brother."

"I know that. And you used to talk about him. When I was little. But then you stopped. It was like you wanted us all to forget him."

"He would be almost sixteen now. Learning how to drive."

Josh went right over and sat next to her.

"I keep track," she said. "I try to picture him, growing up. I can see him so clearly. And sometimes that's almost worse than not seeing him at all."

"Is that why you stopped talking about him? And only have that one photo of him on the wall?"

She looked at Josh quickly and reached over to push back his hair. She told him things, sad things. She said she'd always felt their family was incomplete, and that Josh was missing something. She said that when he had first made up Big Brother, it had been like a dagger to her heart. So she just stopped talking about him, hoping that would keep the imaginary big brother away.

Josh looked over at the photo on the wall, at his mom, so happy with her new baby boy, the one who did not live to his first birthday. He said, "Nothing is missing, Mom."

And they just sat together like that. They didn't say anything, but were both missing him together, each in their own way.

She put her arm around Josh's shoulder and gave him a squeeze. "You're getting so strong, Josh. It must be that bike riding. I'm so proud of you."

"Yeah?"

"Yeah."

She said, "Your dad is coming home tomorrow."

"Really? Tomorrow?"

"I was going to surprise you but—" She shrugged.

Josh almost told her then. He almost told her about the house in the woods, and Lucas Hernandez and Maxie Moon. He almost told her about Big Brother. How he had returned and helped Josh through this time. About his kindness and his cool hair.

But instead he just said this: "Mom, I've been lonely before, but I know I'm not alone." And as soon as he said it, he knew it was true. And he knew it was because of him, Big Brother. And he knew that, even if he never saw him again, he would always feel him close by.

Josh's dad would be home and he wondered if he really would notice the difference in him. Would he be able to see that he'd pushed at his own edges? That he'd become the hero of his own story?

The thing about being the hero is, it doesn't matter. It doesn't matter if anyone else can see it or not. It doesn't matter if anyone believes it or not. It is enough just to be.

Which is exactly what Big Brother had said to him, in so many ways.

Josh still didn't understand how the world worked, any of it, but he knew there was more to it than he could see. Which is why he knew that for the rest of his life, he would carry a ten-dollar bill in a book of poetry with him, just in case he someday met a person named Jackie.

And why he would try to see what was right in front of him, every day. And hopefully that would lead to a banana slug.

He would also look for benches. Benches with names and dates and messages. Benches with plaques written in swirly letters and straight.

Because that's the other thing he learned. Benches were everywhere. They were on cliffs overlooking the ocean, and along hiking trails deep in the woods. They were in city parks and next to shopping malls. And whatever the names and dates on the plaques, whatever the words, each bench really said the same thing:

You were here.

In this world.

And you mattered.

And we miss you.

Instead of a cliff or park or place near a shopping mall, Josh decided he would carry his bench with him. And because he had too many words to ever fit on a plaque, it would just say this:

Thanks, Big Brother. I will never forget.

Acknowledgments:

This started with a ghost story told by my dear friend Steven Hamada. That story led to a trip to Hawaii to research other ghost stories. Thank you Steve, Matthew, and Judy, for making that trip happen. And thanks to everyone who so generously shared homes, meals, and stories: George Masami Tachibana, Florence Satoko Tachibana, Georgiana and Albert Kobayashi (and Chibi), Denise Kutsunai, and Amy Tamura. You helped me understand the ghost stories in my own life, and why I'm drawn to them.

Hello and thanks to Harry Kuboi, wherever you are. And to Guy.

Julie Strauss-Gabel: Thank you for your belief in this story, as well as your clear and bright vision. I'm so glad you saw the gorilla.

Andrew Karre: You are a Zippo lighter in the dark and I'm grateful I had the chance to work with you on this.

So many thanks to everyone at Penguin Young Readers that helped to make this book and get it into the hands of readers, including: Anna Booth, Rob Farren, Melissa Faulner, Maria Fazio, Rosanne Lauer, and Natalie Vielkind.

Liza Pulitzer-Voges: Thank you for your unwavering encouragement and support.

I'm grateful for SCBWI and my writing community. Special thanks this time around to: Dolores Andral, Allison Augustyn, Martha Brockenbrough, Megan Chance, Sarah Conradt-Kroehler, Carol Crews, Wendy Hathaway, Tina Hoggatt, Stephanie Kuehnert Lewis, Maureen Doyle McQuerry, Alix Reid, Kyle Reynolds, Suzanne Selfors, and Jolie Stekly.

Thanks to Lindsey Galovin, Luis Garcia, and Suzie Thomas.

To Simon and Jasper Schwartz: Thank you, lovely sons, for the helpful talks and birthday dinner when I was working to meet a deadline.

And to the marvelous Matthew Reid-Schwartz: Thank you for being the very first member of the Gorilla Club. You win the prize for that, and for everything else.